Rorschach

AARON LEBOLD

Copyright © 2024 by Aaron Lebold
Edited by Heather Ann Larson
Cover design by GetCovers & LM Kaplin
Interior Formatting by LM Kaplin
Published by Broken Brain Books
Paperback ISBN - 979-8-9866751-5-2
First published - September 19th, 2024

This is a work of fiction. Names, characters, places, and incidents either
are the product of the author's imagination or are used fictitiously. Any
resemblance to actual persons, living or dead, events, or locales is entirely
coincidental.

This book is dedicated to anyone who has ever felt the need to make a statement so loud, it would never be forgotten.

RIP Robert 'Budd' Dwyer
November 21, 1939 – January 22, 1987

CHAPTER ONE

SITTING HERE ON THE edge of the overpass, I'm trying to figure out how this whole thing started. I have no idea what time it is, or even what day it is. Looking down, if I had to guess, I would think it's around thirty feet from my dangling toes to the high-traffic freeway. You may be surprised at how many people are out and about at this hour. So many vehicles have gone by that the sound has slowly become white noise. Maybe that has to do with my state of mind.

The breeze is gentle, and it feels good on my skin. I'm not afraid. I'm actually filled with a strange tranquility I can't say I've ever felt. Acceptance. But before I go and do anything I can't take back, perhaps you'll listen to my story? I suppose we may have gotten off on the wrong foot here since I've already lied to you. I'm not trying to figure out how this whole thing started. I know exactly how it started. I remember the day it started. I remember the time it started.

If I haven't lost your trust and you're still willing to hear me out, I'll tell you how it started. I'll tell you everything I can remember about my journey and how I ended up sitting on this overpass at two in the morning on a Tuesday.

CHAPTER TWO

I T WAS JANUARY 22, 1987. I was a young, ambitious journalist working for a small paper in Pennsylvania. I took every story I could to make a name for myself. I felt a passion in writing that helped me feel like I had a purpose. I could use my natural gift of expression to keep the public informed on the latest news.

That day started like any other.

I woke up at around eight and had my coffee. There was a press conference at ten. I knew it would be filled with cameras and journalists, and I saw it as an opportunity to stand out from the competition. From what I understood, it was pretty straightforward. The treasurer, R. Budd Dwyer, had been charged with and convicted of taking bribes from a computer company in a tax refund scheme back in 1984.

Dwyer refused to admit his guilt, but a jury of his peers disagreed. After being found guilty, he was scheduled for sentencing on January 23, the day after his press conference. The event was announced last minute, and nobody seemed to know exactly what he was going to say. There wasn't much doubt the end result was going to be his resignation. I arrived early and still ended up with a mediocre spot in the small room. When Dwyer arrived, he stood behind a large wooden table that separated him from the press.

He started his speech with an obvious animosity. He made accusations about corruption in the court system and continued to proclaim his innocence.

None of the reporters in my immediate vicinity seemed shocked. The guy was looking at some pretty serious jail time. Still, he kept going, and about fifteen minutes in, some of the camera crews started to pack up and leave. I must admit, I thought about doing the same, but really, I didn't have much else on the agenda and I was determined to write the best story I could.

His next words caught my attention. He said, "Those of you who are putting your cameras away, I think you ought to stay because we're not, we're not finished yet."

It wasn't so much what he said, but the way he said it. It sounded like he had something planned. I didn't have to wait long to find out my suspicions were accurate. Dwyer pulled out a gun. Now I know it was a Model 19 .357 Magnum, but at the time, all I could say was it was a gun.

He seemed like he was concerned about the effect it may have on people in the room. He backed himself up against the wall. It was hard to hear him from where I was standing, but later I would learn he said something to the effect of, "Please, please, please leave the room if this will... if this will affect you."

People started to panic. Some ran for the door, and others tried to get the weapon away from him. His final words were directed at those who stood in his way. They weren't of malice but of concern. "Don't, don't, don't, this will hurt someone." A few cameras kept rolling as he slid the gun into his mouth and pulled the trigger. The bullet went through the roof of his mouth and into his brain. He was dead by the time he hit the floor.

Now, this was a true story, and you may have heard it before. January 22, 1987, was in the history books because of a politician shooting himself in front of numerous television cameras. But for me it was the beginning of something. After the press conference was over and I was able to get out of there, I tried to figure out how I would translate my version of the events to paper. Was it still a story about an allegedly corrupt treasurer? It seemed like more than that.

At the time, I had never seen a dead body. I had never seen anyone harm themselves in any way. To say I was traumatized would be an understatement. I walked the streets and tried to reflect. My brain was trying to persuade me to think of the story I was going to write. How was I going to make this thing something that shone the light of good journalism in my direction? That was supposed to be my breakthrough column with the paper.

I sat on a bench outside a store, pulled out my notepad, and jotted down some ideas. I couldn't focus. The sound of the high-powered revolver going off in the small room still echoed in my ears. The sight of pure panic on the faces of people like me and the sinister smiles of those who continued to roll when it was obvious something really awful was about to transpire played on repeat in my head.

Did I fall into the second category? I stuck around even when I felt like something bad might happen. Was that who I wanted to be? Was a story worth it? Would I be able to put my own experience aside and document the facts? I tried to separate the two elements, tried to remove my personal experience and do what I did best. I tried to write and couldn't. My mind kept going to the man himself. He was desperate. Maybe he really was innocent. That angle would split readers, and the paper would never publish it. My personal thoughts and opinions were irrelevant as far as they were concerned.

Then I thought about his family. He mentioned his wife and two children. How was the whole ordeal going to affect them? I sighed and stood from the bench with nothing but scribbles adorning the pages of my notebook. Normally the story would fly out of me at light speed, but that day I wasn't able to tap into it. I questioned everything, but it quickly turned into an internal debate.

Did it make sense to let one traumatic incident change my life? Writing was my passion, and I was good at it. Was I really thinking about throwing away a blooming career because I was questioning the moral integrity of the professionals? Maybe it was a fear I would end up like them. Maybe I was in that room for a reason and it had nothing to do with drafting an eye-catching news article.

I was experiencing a strange confusion I had never felt before. Since high school, I had always known exactly what I wanted to do with my life. I made all the right choices to get me to exactly where I was, and that day was the first time I ever second guessed it. I needed some help. I needed to talk to someone and bounce my thoughts off them. I needed clarity.

I went back to wandering the streets. I had no specific destination, yet somehow I felt myself being gently pulled along. I was in complete control of myself, yet somehow I wasn't. I made a few turns. I wandered down alleys and side streets, parking lots and areas of the city I would normally avoid. I had absolutely no idea what I was looking for until my body stopped mid stride.

I had made my way to a building that sat on a very non-desirable street in a very shady part of town. I was right where your parents warn you to stay away from. The red brick was chipped, and most of the windows were either cracked or boarded up. A neon sign hung in the window. It was supposed to say "Fortunes told" but over half the letters were burned out. I yelled at myself in my mind. *Don't even think about going in there!*

I knocked on the door, and it went slightly ajar. My breathing was heavy and my heart was pounding. I could feel sweat running down my back. But I couldn't get myself to turn around and go home. I pushed on the door and called inside. "Hello? Are you open?" I was pretty certain nobody was in there. I startled a bit when I actually got a response.

"We are open. Please, come inside." It was a raspy woman's voice.

To this day I can't tell you what possessed me to go in that door, but I did. Before I even stepped inside, the smell of rotten wood and must attacked my senses. Part of me was expecting the occupant to be in a similar condition. For a second, it even crossed my mind that

Budd Dwyer himself would be greeting me, the back of his head still blown to pieces.

The room matched the exterior. It looked like it had been abandoned for years. There was very little furniture with the exception of an old couch filled with cobwebs and a brand new desk on the other side of the room. Red Christmas lights had been stapled to the wall to highlight it. My fear dissipated slightly as I felt like I was getting the idea. It was just a cheap gimmick. I had to refocus and reassure myself that my mind had just been playing tricks on me. The new desk and tacky lights were a dead giveaway.

The woman was probably in her thirties. She adorned gypsy garb and had her hands folded on the desk. She was cute, but the whole thing felt like a ruse. She was using the old building for creepy aesthetic and probably had a whole routine worked out. I was about to tell her I was in the wrong store, but she spoke first. "Come inside, I can tell you are troubled. Sit here." She motioned toward an empty chair across from her.

"I don't know. I'm not sure why I even came in here."

"You seek answers, Lucas. You've been brought to me."

I froze for a second. Was she legit? How did she know my name? I glanced down and saw I was still wearing my press pass. "I go by Luke, actually. And you are?"

"Lucas, come sit. My name is Esmerelda."

By that point, I was pretty sure she was a hack. What a cliché name for a cliché gypsy character. "How much is this going to cost me?"

"Sit. Give me ten minutes. If you don't feel that we've connected, then your visit is free."

I couldn't come up with any good reason not to give her ten minutes of my time, so I pulled out the chair and sat across from her. She started with the things you would expect—tarot cards. At the time, I didn't believe in any of that stuff. When she pulled the Death card, I didn't know what it meant but it definitely felt relevant given the day I had. "So, what? I'm going to die?"

She placed the card on the table and ran her long fingernail over the horse-riding skeleton. "This is not a card of death, but life." She locked eyes with me. "Death is a symbol of change. The death of an old life and the rebirth of something new."

I have to admit she had my attention, but I still wasn't convinced. If she had listened to the radio at all she would have heard about Budd Dwyer. She saw my press pass. She clearly had some powers of observation but that didn't make her clairvoyant by any means. It was headline news that the guy shot himself at a press conference that morning, and I was wearing a press pass. Not exactly a pinnacle of detective work.

She picked up on my skepticism. "You are still not convinced. I can show you your future, if you want. I warn you, you can never unsee it."

I rolled my eyes and started to stand. "Well, that's probably close to ten minutes. I'm sorry, but I'm not paying for this."

She put her hand on top of mine. "No charge. I have one more thing to show you. Are you familiar with the Rorschach test?"

I sat back down. "I've never heard of that."

"You likely have. Most call it an inkblot test. I have a method like no other, and I promise you it will give you the answers that you seek."

I sighed. "Alright. Let's do the ink thing, but I need to get going. I have a story to write."

She opened the top drawer of her desk and pulled out three blank cards about the size of a standard piece of paper. I could tell they were porous and designed for a specific purpose. Next she pulled out a small inkwell. She opened the lid and looked at me with a strange anticipation. "For this to work, to really work, I need something from you."

"What?"

"Three drops of your blood."

My immediate reaction was hard to hide. "I'm out of here."

"Luke, you have many questions. You are at an impasse in your life. Three drops of blood will give you all the answers you are seeking. I promise you."

To this day, I can't explain why I considered this. I know I was pretty desperate for clarity and that something had brought me to that place. I reluctantly agreed. She pricked my finger enough that it bled. She gently squeezed three drops into the inkwell.

She mixed the bottle and used a dropper to apply a small amount of ink to each of the textured papers. The ink seemed to spread farther than it should have been able to. A picture emerged on the first one. She looked into my eyes. "What do you see?"

I glanced down, and an image became apparent. "It's some kind of hat. Like someone would wear at a high school graduation."

She pushed the first card to the side as the second took shape. She locked eyes with me again. "Here?"

"I see a telephone."

She nodded and slid the second paper to the side. The third spread. She looked at me again, this time without words.

I found everything about the experience rather unnerving, but I couldn't look away. The final paper was a little unsettling. "I see a man holding a noose. There is another man there, offering his hand."

She nodded and collected her cards. "Thank you for your time, Lucas. Your destiny will soon become clear."

I left that place feeling more confused than I felt going in. I went back to my apartment and tried to sleep, but the images from the cards kept appearing in my head. I had a moment of clarity. From the first and third images, I deduced I was supposed to go back to school and learn how to help people that were struggling with thoughts of suicide. I couldn't place the second, but it was hard to convince myself I hadn't had a life-changing epiphany.

The next morning before going to work, I made my way back to the building. I wanted to share the news with the gypsy woman that she helped me realize what I needed to do. When I got there it looked the same, but the neon sign was gone. I knocked on the door, and again it opened from the force, but I heard no welcome.

"Hello? You here?"

Nothing. I went in to see everything was the same except the desk. Now it looked just as old and weathered as everything else. The lights were gone, and there were no signs of the woman. On the desk sat the three pieces of blotter paper and the inkwell. The papers were all blank. I wasn't sure what to do, and I questioned my sanity.

For some reason, one which I still don't know, I took the papers and the ink. Of all the things I've ever done in my life, that was the one I question the most. Whatever my motives were, I did it. I put them in my bag and left the building, unsure of whether I was stealing or taking something I was supposed to have. I vowed to never go back.

CHAPTER THREE

I WAS NEVER WHAT you would call an impulsive person. I've heard people say they "found their calling," and until that time in my life, I never really understood what it meant. I found mine in 1987. I approached my boss and quit my job at the newspaper. He tried to convince me to at least write the article on Dwyer's press conference, but I told him I couldn't. I knew I couldn't be objective, and besides, everyone was covering that. A few stations even played the uncensored footage on television.

I left the office with no job and a vague idea that I wanted to go back to school and get myself into some type of social services. For some reason, the image of the graduation cap kept flashing in my head. The Rorschach test.

The month that followed was a bit surreal. I found myself going to all the right places and meeting all the right people. I felt compelled by something. It was similar to the feeling I had as I wandered toward that abandoned building on January 22. The building that changed my entire life.

I enrolled in school for social services. I spent three years in that course and earned a Bachelor's degree. I had almost forgotten about the other inkblot cards until it was time to choose a placement. Every student needed to work in the field for six months to gain some experience. I had no idea where I wanted to end up until I noticed there was an option to work at a suicide hotline.

The phone. I decided right away I was going to go in that direction. Working with people who were in crisis was exactly what I wanted to do; what was better than a suicide hotline? I wouldn't say the recollection of the Rorschach was the only reason I chose that placement, but it certainly didn't seem like a coincidence.

I vividly remember my first day. I met with the supervisor, Nancy. She came across as a little stressed and a little impatient. I could tell right away she had a lot of years in the field and had grown a bit jaded. Don't get me wrong, she was nice, but she had a very busy feel to her. She was around thirty-five but looked at least forty-five. She had a beautiful dark complexion made less attractive by the dark circles under her eyes and frown lines.

She set me up with someone from the administration office, and we reviewed all the policies and procedures. I wasn't sure what I was expecting, but I was a bit disappointed to be starting on the sidelines. For the rest of the week, all I was allowed to do was watch. I was paired with a man named Chad. It was set up so I could listen to his calls on a headset, and I was supposed to take notes of the things I learned, what techniques he used, that sort of thing.

Chad had a sophisticated look to him. His hair was dark and straight, and he always wore a suit. His shoes were always shining. I found this a bit strange since nobody outside the office would ever see us. He stood out from everyone else who dressed more casually. Most of our conversations were work related, but after a couple of days, I had to ask him. "Hey, Chad. Why do you dress like a businessman?"

He didn't seem put off by my question. He actually seemed eager to answer. Maybe he had been waiting for me to ask. He straightened his tie and looked me in the eyes. "I remember when I was where you're at, Luke."

"I actually go by Lucas these days."

"Well, there you go. Then you know why I dress like this. I'm a professional. Lucas is a much more professional name than Luke now, isn't it?"

I hadn't really put much thought into it. "I suppose. Yes."

"As soon as you get comfortable, you stop growing. This job is great. It'll teach you things that school never could. You'll be facing difficult questions and you'll have to face the reality that you can't help everyone."

I nodded. He had my full attention.

"As soon as things start to feel easy, it's time to challenge yourself. You met Nancy?"

"Yeah."

"Could you tell how burned out she is?"

I wasn't sure how to answer that. I was pretty sure it was bad practice to call your boss a burnout on your first week. "She looks like she's experienced."

He chuckled. "I like the way you put that. Yes, experienced. Now, is that where you want to find yourself in twenty years? Obviously experienced?"

I shook my head. I still tried to tread lightly, but the things Chad was saying made sense.

"Someone like her, she got into this job and stayed. When things got easy, she let them be easy. You see it all the time. People start dressing like they're out with friends and they lose track of their professionalism. I dress like this so I never forget my goals. I'm back in school to get my masters. I'm never going to stop. I will never allow myself to become complacent."

That conversation really stuck out to me. Chad made something that was often mocked by his peers into something that made total sense. Really, fuck what people think. You need to do what feels right to you if you want to get to where you want to be. I decided in that moment I was going to do the same. I would take everything I could from that position and use it to propel myself forward.

I listened in on Chad's calls for almost two weeks. He was very professional, and he showed exceptional empathy. He had a way about him that made people really listen, even when they were debating their own existence. He always kept calm and would stick to a similar script.

"What can you tell me about how you're feeling?" "How do you think the people in your life would feel if they lost you?" Things like that. Open-ended questions that encouraged the caller to reflect on things. Before any of that, he would always ask if they had a plan. If they did, he would prod about how feasible it was. If a guy said he was going to blow his head off, he would ask if he had a gun. If he didn't have one, it became apparent he was more looking for help than an excuse to die.

Soon enough, I found myself taking calls. Each call had to be recorded, and I was very nervous the first time. A man called who couldn't stop drinking. He had lost his wife, his house, his kids, everything. I used a lot of the techniques I learned from Chad and ended up convincing the man to go to a treatment center. The tricky part about that job was you typically never heard how things turned out.

I took that first call as a win, but for all I knew, the guy stepped into traffic on the way to detox. I never really considered that back then, though. Calls kept getting easier for me as I learned how to communicate with people in crisis. I found myself wearing dress shirts to work and shining my shoes. I never went to a suit and tie like Chad did, but I dabbled in his ideas. I had to admit, it probably helped me feel, and in turn, act more confident and professional.

By the time I was working on the last month of my placement, I felt pretty confident. I debated applying for a full-time position and sticking with the bachelor's degree. But something nagged at me from the depths of my mind. Maybe it was all the things Chad had said about getting complacent and never going any further on your journey. I tried to ignore it, but the feelings continued to intensify.

Chad and I had become fairly close during my placement. Not close enough that we hung out on the weekends, but close enough we would share work details with each other. I noticed Chad had at least three calls where the person killed themselves while he was still on the phone with them. I was always a bit surprised at how well he handled it. I figured he just learned to separate himself from the inevitable tragedies of the work we did.

I got heavier feelings as the days passed. Feelings I couldn't quite place but that didn't seem to want to atrophy. I racked my brain trying to sort through them, but I kept going back to the idea of one solution. I needed to use the cards again. They gave me clarity when I needed it most and basically guided me to where I needed to be.

One night after work, I decided I was going to go for it. I made it back to my apartment and pulled the papers and ink from the drawer I had stashed them in back when I first started school. I placed them on the table and stared at them. It was hard not to question your own sanity when you were looking at an inkwell and some paper and thinking you were going to get some actual resolve.

I grabbed a small knife from my kitchen drawer and sat down at the table. I lifted my hand to my face and stared at it. The gypsy woman needed my blood, so I figured it probably wouldn't work without it. I pressed the tip of the blade against my index finger and applied just enough pressure that it broke the skin. Blood drawn, I placed my finger over the inkwell. One, two, three drops. Just like the woman needed.

I set down the knife and picked up the ink, giving it a swirling stir. I tried to mimic exactly what I had seen from the best of my recollection. I tipped the bottle over the first paper and allowed a single drop to fall. Then the second and the third. An image formed on the first paper. I set down the ink and lifted the paper to see what it was going to tell me.

It was a magnifying glass. I thought that to be a bit strange, but it was clear as day what the image was. I set the paper down and picked up the second. The ink was spreading around and soaking in to form another image. It was a bottle and a steering wheel. Again, strange.

I repeated the process again with the third paper. My eyes widened as it became clear. It was a perspective image. It was a first-person view of a hand holding a large object. I thought it looked like a rock but couldn't say for sure. I set down the paper and covered my face with my hands to try to think. A magnifying glass, a bottle with a steering wheel, and a man holding a rock. I again thought I was losing my mind. On the other hand, the Rorschach worked.

I rubbed my eyes and took my hands off my face. When I looked down, I saw once again the three papers were blank. At that point, I felt like a lunatic. The Rorschach did work, didn't it? I knew it did. I knew what I saw, but I didn't know what it meant. I thought back to my experience with the gypsy. I didn't know what they meant at the time back then, either, but over time, they made sense.

I put the papers and ink back in the drawer and decided I needed to get some sleep. I hoped things would make more sense in the morning.

CHAPTER FOUR

W HEN I WOKE IN the morning, I decided I was
going to try to forget everything about the night
before. I sang a stupid earworm song from the early
eighties every time I needed to drown out any thoughts
of the images I was sure I saw. I did see them, right? "It's
the... eye of the tiger it's the thrill of the fight..." I needed
to stay grounded, to stay in reality.

When I got to work, I was greeted by Chad. I was a bit
surprised since he worked late the night before. "Hey
man. You're here early."

He ran his fingers through his dark hair and
straightened his tie, telltale signs he was uncomfortable.
"Yeah, well, I had another boomer last night after you
left."

"Boomer?"

"Yeah. He had a gun, and I couldn't stop him. Boom."

It took me a second to process what I was hearing. "He
shot himself?"

"Yep. I came in early to do some paperwork. Besides,
it's hard to be at home sometimes when things like that
happen on your shift. How was your night?"

I tried so hard to keep the inkblots out of my head. Serious red flags jumped at me about Chad, and all I could see was the magnifying glass. I needed to investigate. "Oh, it was OK. Just watched some TV and went to bed early."

Chad nodded and patted me on the shoulder. "Right on, Lucas. Anyway, see you at lunch. Don't do anything I wouldn't do." He smirked before walking toward his desk.

For some reason, that interaction put Chad in a whole different light for me. I couldn't place it, but I felt compelled to go with my instincts. Again, it was like some sort of external force was pushing me. It pushed me right to Nancy's office. I knocked twice.

"Make it quick." Her voice was muffled through the door.

I went inside and thought on my feet. "Hey. So, I'm almost done here, and I was hoping to make sure I was learning as much as I could about the process."

"Right. Glad to see you taking some initiative. What are you thinking?"

"We record all the calls, right?"

"Yeah."

"Well, Chad said he had a bad one yesterday. I was hoping I could listen to it and see what happened. I haven't had one yet myself, and I want to see if I can see any signs or things I may have done differently."

She nodded. "His report says he hit the wrong button when the call started and it didn't record, but you're welcome to review some of the others. It happens more often than we would like it to."

My suspicion spiked. I had no reason to think Chad was doing something unethical, but I couldn't shake the feeling something was off. "I would love to hear some tapes."

She reached into her desk drawer and pulled out a set of keys. She fumbled through them until she found the one she was looking for. She reached out with them in her hands but paused before dropping them into mine. "Obviously I don't need to tell you that this is for educational purposes only and you are not to discuss what you hear with anyone outside of the organization."

"Obviously. Thank you. I appreciate all you've done for me here."

"The files are in the storage room down the hall and to your left. Close the door on your way out."

I gave a slight nod and made sure to close the door as I left. I went down to the storage room. There were filing cabinets lining the walls; there must have been thousands of tapes in that room. I just hoped I would know where to look to find whatever it was I wasn't sure I was looking for.

I figured I would just dive in and start looking. It didn't take long to figure out the filing system. Each file had cassettes from specific days as well as the report that went with it. I found a few of Chad's calls, but nothing stood out until I came across another one that hadn't been recorded. I glanced at the report; it said the machine had eaten the tape.

There were a couple that were recorded, and I took some time to listen to them. Everything seemed pretty legitimate. Chad did everything he could to save the caller, but their mind seemed to be already made up.

I poked around in that room for hours and ended up finding four separate occasions where Chad had lost a caller and the conversation hadn't been recorded, always explained by technical issues or human error. With the one that occurred the night before, that put five deaths on his watch.

Given the nature of our clientele, it wasn't really that shocking, but my doubt increased and drove me to keep pushing. I was taking a short break from my investigation when the door opened. I instinctively jumped, startled. Nancy came into the room. "How are things going? I need to go to a meeting soon, so I'm going to need you to clean up in here and give me back the keys."

I nodded. "Sure thing." I felt like I needed to dig deeper on Chad, but I didn't know what to ask. "Hey, how is Chad doing?"

She shrugged. "Fine. He's always fine."

"Does that come over time? You get used to death?"

"Some do. Chad's been used to death since before he ever started here. I was a bit surprised that he was even interested in this job."

I felt like this was an angle I hadn't considered. "What do you mean?"

Nancy sighed. "Look, between you and me, Chad lost both of his parents a few years ago. They were hit by a drunk driver and ended up burning to death in their car. He never talks about it, but I'm sure it fuels his need to help other people who are struggling."

The image of the bottle and the steering wheel jumped directly into my mind. The accident must be relevant. I started putting all the files away to keep myself grounded. "That's really sad."

"Yeah. I'll need those keys back in ten minutes."

I nodded. "I'll be done by then. Thanks again for letting me check them out, I learned a lot."

She nodded and left the room, closing the door behind her. I moved quickly to put the room back the way it had been when I found it, then locked it up. On my way back to Nancy's office, I ran into Chad. My heart sped up, and it must have been obvious.

"Hey man, you okay?"

I wiped the sweat off my forehead. "Yeah, just have to get these keys back to Nancy before her meeting."

"Keys? Did I just see you come out of the storage room? What are you doing in there?"

My voice was a bit shaky and I wasn't sure why. "Yeah, just trying to learn more before I finish up here. Listening to some calls where the people didn't make it. I haven't had one yet, myself."

Chad squinted slightly, and I could tell he was suspicious of something. "You listen to any of mine?"

I shrugged. "One, I think. There was another I looked at, but I guess you had some issues with the machine and it didn't record."

He nodded. "Yeah, happens sometimes. You better get those keys back."

I walked past him, and he didn't move. It seemed like some kind of intimidation tactic. I tried to ignore it as I went to Nancy's office to return the keys. As soon as I left, I saw Chad standing there again like he was waiting for me.

"Does that seem weird to you? That my tape recorder didn't work?"

I shrugged. "I could see it happening. Mind if I ask what your caller last night was upset about?"

His eyes widened. "Sure, man. The guy had run over some kid while he was driving drunk. He never got caught and he couldn't live with the guilt. What do you say to someone like that?"

I tried to keep an unassuming look. The fact the caller had been driving drunk certainly fit with Chad's past. "I'm not sure. I know I would feel horrible if that ever happened to me."

"It didn't happen to him. It happened because of him. It happened because he made the decision to get hammered and drive his car."

A strange tension filled the air, and I wasn't sure what to say. It was becoming clear Chad wasn't over what happened to his parents. I thought maybe he was being some kind of vigilante and pushing people like that to the edge. Over the edge. Using his job and his communication skills to exact some kind of revenge.

His face went back to normal in the wake of the silence. "Hey, Lucas, want to go for a walk with me after work? May be better than just going home and watching TV like you always do."

I felt a bit suspicious of his invitation, but my instincts were telling me to keep moving and see what he may have planned. "Sure man, I'd like that. Where do you want to go?"

He placed his hand on my shoulder again. "You'll see. I'm going to take you somewhere that helps me clear my head every time the job gets stressful." He nodded at me before heading back to work.

I went back and took a few calls, but it was hard to stay focused. I watched the hands on the clock move one tick at a time. The sound amplified in my ears as I counted down the minutes. Eventually the inevitable happened and the work day came to an end. As I was cleaning up my workstation and printing my reports, I looked up to see Chad standing over me.

"Ready to go?"

"Yep. Just finishing up these reports and I'm all set. Where are we going? I can meet you there."

"I'll drive." He made his way to the door and waited for me like an eager child.

I tried my best not to act nervous as I fumbled with my paperwork and made my way over to meet him. He held the door for me and led the way to his car. He pointed to a blue Chevette. "There she is. Hop in."

Without a word, I reached for the door handle. I could tell my hands were shaking, and I kept asking myself what I was doing. I wondered if Ted Bundy's victims felt the same way as they reached for the handle of his yellow Volkswagen.

"Buckle up." He had a grin on his face as he loosened his tie. I complied with his request, and we started driving. It wasn't long before we pulled over on the side of the road, near a forest. "This is it."

"Where are we?"

"This is Devil's Canyon." He pointed to his left. "There's a trailhead a ways up the road, but I found a quicker way in. Spending time in the forest and seeing this beautiful view always grounds me when things feel heavy." He looked at me with an unsettling affect. "I feel like things are feeling heavy for you right now, Lucas."

I nodded. At least I didn't have to lie. "They are."

He opened his door and got out, waving for me to follow him. All my instincts were screaming at me to run, but the strange energy I felt from the Rorschach seemed to be pushing me forward. I got out and followed him into the forest. We walked down a trail likely made by animals and didn't talk for at least twenty minutes.

When we came to a clearing, he stretched his arms out wide. "There she is, Devil's Canyon."

It was a beautiful sight. We must have been close to two hundred feet up, and you could see everything. With my eyes locked on the majesty of nature, I nearly fell on my face as I tripped over a rock.

Chad took notice. "Be careful there, Luke. It would be pretty easy for a man to fall to his death from this height."

I could feel myself becoming guarded as he spoke.

"You know, Luke... Sometimes I think that there are people out there who deserve to die. What do you think?"

I knew whatever he had planned was starting, and I tried to keep it together. "I don't know, maybe. Like who?"

He smiled. "You know who. Drunks. People that operate vehicles when they can barely walk. People that don't think twice about the consequences of their actions. I know you've been thinking something unflattering about the way I operate. For some reason I even felt like you may have been looking into me today when you were locked up in that back room."

I tried to play dumb. "What do you mean?"

"I know you figured it out, Luke." I wasn't sure if he was using my old name as some sort of psychological trick or what, but it was working. He turned and looked over the canyon. "Yeah, those calls were missed on purpose. Yeah, those people died because I decided that they should. So what are you going to do with this information?"

"Nothing."

"Right. Let me just make something clear here, Luke. A man could easily fall off this ledge, and the cops would call it an accident. Understand?"

I felt something come over me. Something powerful. The fact this man was using his own trauma to excuse being a mass murderer of sorts was something I couldn't ignore. I looked at my feet and saw the rock I had nearly tripped on. I looked up at him. His suit and tie and fancy shoes no longer seemed professional. They seemed like a costume. He still had his back to me when I picked up the rock.

He turned to face me at the same time I swung it. The inkblot picture appeared in front of me as I saw my hand holding a rock and smashing into another man's face. It happened too quickly but also felt like slow motion. His forehead split open like warm bread, and his eyes rolled back in his head.

He did a deadfall straight backward off the side of the canyon, and I glanced over the edge to see his body smashing off the edges of the cliff and flailing around like a rag doll. When he hit the ground, I could hear the impact echoing through the beautiful space. It was more of a crunching noise than a splatting noise, and on impact, his body created a giant splash of red on the rocks.

I looked in my hand and saw the rock had blood on it. I tossed it over the edge and examined myself for any evidence. Back then, forensics wasn't what it was now, and I wasn't too concerned. There was some blood on the ground that spurted from his head between the impact of the rock and his swan dive. I kicked the dirt, and it sounded like rain as it fell to the ground below.

I wish I could say I felt horrible for what I had done, but I didn't. I did start to feel more like myself, though, like whatever was urging me on had dissipated. I collected my thoughts and made my way back through the game trail and to the road. His car was still there; I figured that was a good thing. I made my way back to the office on foot.

It was around that time I decided I needed to push forward with life. The suicide hotline gig had taught me a lot of things on a lot of levels, but I decided not to stay. I would finish my placement, then go back to school to earn my master's degree. Chad's body was found a couple days later when someone reported his Chevette had been left on the side of the road. His death was ruled accidental, and I was never questioned.

CHAPTER FIVE

MY FIRST DAY BACK at university was another notable day. I was starting a course on human behavior and got there a bit early. The lecture hall began to fill up, but I didn't really notice anyone until she walked in. Of course, there is always a "she." I found out her name was Claire Stewart. Of all the empty seats, she came and sat beside me. Maybe it was fate. Maybe it was bad luck. Sometimes the two were easy to confuse.

She was radiant. She had her hair dyed blue, and she wore a hoop in her nose. She had the most radiant hazel eyes, and at first glance I swore I could see her soul. And, at the risk of sounding shallow, she had a great figure. She presented immediately as independent, like she had the same attitude as me about society and life. I felt nervous when she first sat down, but something about the way she spoke put me at ease almost immediately.

"Hey, here to learn about humans?"

I tried to keep cool. "Yeah, so far all I know is that I hate them."

"They are the worst. You want to be a shrink?"

I scoffed. "No way. I was thinking high school guidance counselor. I've set my bar pretty high."

She looked so beautiful when she smiled. The lesson started, and I did my best to pay attention. I found myself looking at her in regular intervals. Once I caught myself doing it, I worried I was coming off as some kind of weirdo. I made a conscious effort to stop, but once I did, I caught her doing the same from my peripheral.

I may not have absorbed a lot of information from that class, but I did acquire a feeling I had never experienced. I felt a chemistry between us after a single encounter. It was so overwhelming I did something I had never done before. Once class was over and people started leaving the room, I asked her out. I could barely look at her. "Hey, Claire." I felt her eyes on me. "Do you maybe want to go for dinner or something with me?"

That was the first and only time I ever understood what it meant to have butterflies in your stomach. It was a different feeling from adrenaline. It was stronger than the feelings I had right before I pushed Chad off Devil's Canyon.

I could tell she was feeling it too, which was why her response was as much of a shock as it was a disappointment. "I would love to, Lucas. Believe me, I would. It's just... my ex-boyfriend would be really mad at me."

"Your ex-boyfriend? Doesn't that imply past tense?"

She became very awkward. "Yeah, well, we still sort of live together. It's complicated. I'm sorry, I have to go." She turned quickly and didn't look back as she walked out of the room.

As I watched her leave, I smiled. I knew it was far from over. I wasn't sure why, but somehow I had come to truly believe in the forces I was feeling. I was being guided by something. Maybe it was the universe, maybe it was God, maybe it was the Rorschach. Whatever it was, it didn't matter. I didn't need to identify it, I just needed to feel it, to trust it, and to believe it. I did wholeheartedly, with absolutely no tangible proof it existed. I guess that's what they called faith.

As the weeks went on, we continued to sit next to each other in that particular class. It was strange; sometimes I found myself saying things I had never even thought of. There were times where I almost felt like I was watching my own life through a different lens, like everything outside my head was a TV show and I was just a spectator taking notes from the couch. That may sound crazy, and maybe it was. On the other hand, maybe it was a gift. Either way, it was working.

I learned her ex-boyfriend's name was Keith. He was controlling and could get abusive. She had ended the relationship several times, but he never acknowledged it. He would do whatever he wanted, sleep with whoever he wanted, but expected Claire to be there when he called. It turned out it wasn't the first relationship of that nature she had been involved in, and her biggest motivator for learning about the human mind was to try to understand her own patterns.

Once she opened up to me about the general story, she shared more details about her daily life. We started talking on the phone, but she would often have to hang up mid sentence if Keith came home. She was petrified of him, and she was legitimately concerned that if she tried to leave, he would kill her. It was hard to know what to say to someone in that situation, but I did my best to be supportive. I could tell she appreciated it.

I remained cautious about interfering. It wasn't really my business, and to be honest, the guy sounded a little intimidating. My feelings for Claire continued to intensify, and when she showed up to class one day with a black eye, I felt a rage flow through me. She didn't want to talk about it, so I didn't press the issue. I did my best to clarify I was there if she needed me and that I would stay objective. That night, she called me.

"Lucas, I feel so stupid. I don't know what to do." She was in tears.

"You're not stupid, Claire. People get trapped in these kinds of relationships more often than you think. Want to tell me what happened?"

"Not really. It's embarrassing. When I say it out loud, I know that the person I'm talking to is wondering why I put up with it. Wondering why I don't just leave. I wonder the same thing sometimes."

I took a deep breath and pondered my reaction. I knew what I wanted to say but didn't think I should. I kept with the supportive approach. "I won't judge you. Maybe hearing it out loud will help you put things in perspective."

"He came home." She started sobbing. "He was drunk." She tried to control her tears. "He told me he tried to call and I didn't answer. He said he knew it was because I had some guy over. He called me a slut and punched me in the ribs. He always hits me where people won't see it." She took a deep breath. "I tried to run and smashed my face off an open cabinet in the kitchen."

"I'm so sorry, Claire." My mind was fixed on the inkblots, but I wasn't sure why. "Is there anything I can do?"

"No. I have to do this myself. I just need some kind of sign. Some kind of guidance. I need to know where--" She hung up.

I put the phone back on the hook and sat on the couch. I felt bad for her, but I also really wanted her in my life. I wished I could switch bodies with her for just long enough that I could smash Keith in the face with something.

I obviously knew that wasn't a feasible option. I pulled the inkwell from the drawer and stared at it. I had never done the test on someone else before and had no idea if it would even work.

Then I thought it was quite possible it had never worked at all and I had been slowly losing it. Maybe I wanted to try it on her for my own peace of mind. If she saw pictures on the cards, then they were really there. If they disappeared into thin air after she saw them, she could at least confirm I wasn't a complete nutcase. Maybe they would help her. I couldn't help but feel they were my first thought for a reason.

She never called me back that night. I waited up in the hope she would, and my concern grew with every silent hour. Sometimes my mind lured me into this chaotic abyss of worst-case scenarios. Back then I had a harder time controlling it, and that night was pretty rough. By the time I was on my way to school, I was expecting to see the flag at half mast.

I was relieved to see it wasn't, but it didn't do much to sedate my overall concern. I made it to class at least a half hour early and waited for her to show up. When she finally did, she didn't even want to look at me.

"I was hoping you would call me back last night." I knew she felt my eyes on her.

"Sorry," she replied, staring at the floor.

"Are you alright?"

"I'm fine." She looked flat. Emotionless. Defeated.

"I was thinking about what you said. About wanting some guidance."

Finally, she locked eyes with me. "If you're going to tell me to leave him, save it." She was talking in a whisper, but her tone was a scream.

I tried not to take it personally. "I have an idea. It's a bit unorthodox, but if you trust me, we can try it."

She still had a guarded look on her face, but underneath I could see the real her. The part of her that was still open to being vulnerable. The part of her that had hope. I could tell she was considering asking for more information, and in that moment, I hoped and prayed I was making the right decision.

"What is it?"

I looked at the clock. I needed to kill some time and make sure I wanted to follow through. "Can you come back to my apartment after school? All I need is ten minutes and an open mind."

"I'll think about it."

Her optimism was hidden under a blanket of embarrassment and mistrust. I could see it. No, I could feel it. I knew part of her was wondering if I was trying to get to her back to my place to take advantage of her or make some kind of sexual advance. Part of her was hopeful that maybe I had some sort of solution. Most of her was afraid. Afraid to venture into the unknown, afraid to put any real trust in another living person. I understood that and accepted her answer to think about it. The professor started the class, and I let it be.

I went through the rest of the day as usual, trying not to overthink. I tapped into my new way of thinking. I had faith things would turn out how they were supposed to. She would meet me after school and I would help her get some clarity, or she wouldn't. If she didn't, my instincts were wrong. I realized there was no point in stressing over things beyond my control. I did my best to take everything in stride and trust the process.

That got me through the day. Once my last class let out, I couldn't control my nerves. I could feel my heart beating through my chest and I wasn't sure why. Claire was my friend. Was she destined to be more than that? Was this day a make it or break it kind of deal? Too many thoughts to be able to listen to. Goddamn this noise inside my head.

I did some deep breathing and tried to focus. I waited around for a few minutes before deciding she had decided to opt out. I couldn't blame her. What could someone like me possibly have to offer? What did I have to offer? I headed toward home.

"Lucas!"

The sound of her voice sent a warm wave up my entire body. I turned around to see her keeping a quick pace and heading toward me. In that brief moment, I wondered how a woman I barely knew managed to get such a hold on me.

"Wait up." She sounded a bit out of breath. "Okay, here's the deal. I'll come back with you, but no funny stuff. I don't need any more complications in my life. Deal?"

I nodded. "Absolutely."

She didn't even ask what I had planned until we made it back to my apartment. The walk there was mostly silent. She was probably feeling just as overwhelmed as I was even though there was seemingly no logical reason. We got back to my apartment and headed inside.

Claire was the first person I allowed into my personal space. I had never even thought of that when I invited her over. It was my sanctuary. I hoped I knew what I was doing. I motioned toward my kitchen table. "Have a seat." I headed to the drawer where I kept the paper and inkwell.

"Okay, so I'm listening. What's your plan to help things make sense?"

I walked over to the table and laid down the three blank pieces of blotter paper. I pulled out the inkwell. "Have you ever heard of a Rorschach test?""

"Seriously? Like inkblots? That's your big idea?"

Despite her skepticism, I knew my biggest hurdle was just over the horizon. "Look, I know it sounds crazy, but you have to trust me. I need a few drops of your blood in this ink."

"What the fuck?"

"I know. Listen, I've done this before. Worst case scenario, you get no real answers and you're just back where you are now."

"Except I'll be missing some blood." She was understandably apprehensive, but I could see a spark of curiosity flickering behind her eyes. "Fuck it. Okay."

I nodded and pulled the same knife I used on myself from the kitchen drawer. I sat down across from her. "Give me your hand." She complied. I poked the tip of the blade gently into her skin until a spot of blood appeared. Placing the ink bottle underneath, I gently squeezed and we simultaneously counted three drops.

I swirled the bottle, then tilted it enough for a single drop to fall onto each piece. This was my moment. She would see images and create a brand new compass for her life, or she would see nothing and I could rest assured I was insane. I watched her eyes fix on the first sheet.

"Holy shit."

CHAPTER SIX

IT WAS MY FIRST time doing the test with someone else. My initial thought was I was a loon and she was going to be disappointed. I saw nothing on the first sheet. Claire couldn't take her eyes off of it.

"What do you think that is?"

"You see something?"

"You don't?"

"No. I was expecting you to get up and leave. What do you see?"

She went silent and her eyes moved to the second paper. I could tell she was in deep thought by the time she moved to the third. She looked up at me, and for the first time since I had met her, I saw hope in her eyes. "That is unbelievable. You don't see that? Where did you get these?"

I shrugged. "Long story that you probably wouldn't believe. What do you see?"

"The first one looks just like my teddy bear. The one I cry to and the one I talked to before I met you. Sounds crazy, I know."

"At this point, there isn't much that could sound crazy to me with regards to those papers. What else?"

"It's a pair of handcuffs in the second and a flying bird in the third. What does it mean?"

"I think that's up to you to figure out. Feel any better?"

She still had a dazed look on her face. "Yeah... I think I do." She stood from the chair and offered me a hug. We had never had any physical contact before, and her embrace felt like a warm slice of perfection. I squeezed tightly. For comfort reasons, or course. She then kissed me on the cheek, and without any more words, she left my apartment.

The rest of the night left me with a strange combination of clarity and further confusion. She saw something in those cards I couldn't. I even went to the library and tried to search for the origin of them. I found the concept was created by Leonardo da Vinci in the nineteenth century. Later, Hermann Rorschach took it a step further by doing official tests, which were accompanied by a book of his findings. Fascinating, right? Still didn't explain the test sitting on my table.

I tried to sleep but found myself getting up regularly to go look at the papers. They were blank every time. I wanted to call Claire, but I didn't want to be the cause of any disruption at her place. I didn't know if Keith was home or how he may respond to a male caller. All I could do was try to sleep. I may have gotten three hours in short intervals.

The next morning, I was early again to school and to my first class. No sign of Claire. I waited with anticipation, and by the time the lecture started, I was pretty close to panic mode. I did my best to pay attention but kept looking at the door and hoping she was just running behind. She didn't show up.

Once class was over, I debated skipping the rest of the day to go check in on her, but again my concern was still the same. Her life was difficult enough without me randomly showing up and making it worse. I tried to clear my mind of her, the test, and all the dreadful possibilities, but that was a lot easier in theory.

I decided to go home and try to relax. Again, this was a lot easier in theory. I flicked through the channels but couldn't get my mind off Claire. Not knowing what was going on was destroying me, and I found myself wondering why that woman was so important to me. I watched the clock for a couple of hours until I heard a knock on my door. My heart raced with anticipation as soon as the sound of knuckles connecting with wood hit my ears.

I jumped up and went over. In that brief moment, I pondered all the possible outcomes. Was it Claire? Was it Keith? The police? I took a deep breath as I reached for the handle. I felt an enormous sense of relief when I opened it to see Claire standing on the other side. Before I could ask her any questions, she bounced across the threshold and wrapped her arms around me. She started sobbing within moments.

"Are you alright?" I held her close but tried to stay friendly. She sobbed a bit harder. "It's alright." I gave her a minute to cry before she pulled away.

"Sorry to just show up like this." She wiped her eyes. "Sorry I'm a mess. What a day, you wouldn't believe it."

"No need to apologize, I'm so glad to see you. I've been really worried. What happened?"

Her eyes lit up. They were red, but otherwise you wouldn't have known she had just been sobbing uncontrollably. "The Rorschach. It came true. All of it."

I tilted my head and pointed to the couch. "Please, come in and sit down. You have me intrigued."

She nodded and followed me over to the couch. She sat down with a heavy flop and took an exaggerated, deep breath. "Okay." She took another breath, slightly less heavy. "So, I went home last night and Keith was pissed that I was late. He was questioning me and smashing things around. I thought of my bear and tried to talk to it to calm down. He kicked in the bedroom door, and I ended up going out the window."

"Oh my god, that sounds horrible. Are you alright?"

She put up her hand. "I wasn't at the time, but yeah. Anyways, I ran and hid near a tree. I was in a rough state, so I talked to my bear. I said a lot. I said everything. Soon enough, he found me and dragged me back inside."

"So far this doesn't sound good at all."

"I know, just listen. So that was the first card, right? My bear? So anyways, things kept going bad for a bit until there was a knock on the door. It turned out to be the cops. One of the neighbors had overheard me talking and called for a wellness check. He got arrested for domestic assault."

"That's great! So he's gone?"

"Yeah, but listen. So, that was the second card, right? Handcuffs? I was still a bit skeptical and thought it was just a coincidence, until the next day. I was up super late dealing with everything and didn't get up until the afternoon. The first thing I saw when I got up was a bird fly by my window. I know that could be another coincidence, but it was the exact same shape as the one from the test. It was the same bird. Those tests predicted my future!"

The excitement radiating off her was contagious. I wasn't surprised at the results of the test, but I was certainly a lot more confident in my own sanity. I decided I would tell her the story about the day I got them. I shared about Budd Dwyer and how I ended up in a strange little fortune-telling shop in the ghetto. She actually listened with fascination instead of the skepticism I expected. I decided not to mention the second test I had done on myself. Being weird may be something people could overlook, but being a murderer was a different story.

She ended up staying the night. It was one of the best nights of my life. We talked about everything. She was so much more open about her life and her history with Keith. It seemed like she had found a liberation she hadn't experienced before with him being locked up. She felt safe. That night, I became her boyfriend. Yes, we slept together, and it was everything I hoped it would be.

The next morning, we woke up and had coffee together before going to school as a couple. It felt so natural, like we already had a routine even though it was the first time it happened. Everything about Claire felt right, and I didn't want to let it go. When she asked me about moving in, it felt like an easy question.

It turned out the apartment she shared with Keith was in his name. He controlled everything, and she had been feeling like a prisoner. With him in jail, we went over after school and collected the few belongings she had left. She had a little hideaway spot with some cash and pictures of her family. Even with all of her clothes, all we ended up collecting was a single garbage bag of her things. Of course, her bear was in that bag.

Things were going picture perfect for the next three weeks. We never got sick of each other and we never fought. If we did disagree, we seemed to have a natural knack for being able to work things out. There were a couple times she asked me about the tests. She thought it was a fun idea to see the future. This was our biggest disagreement and the only secret I kept from her.

I didn't know for sure the tests had anything to do with Chad's death. Maybe I would have pushed him anyway, but I wasn't sure. That's not the sort of thing you want to mess around with. The energy that consumed me and compelled me on that day was so strong, I often wondered if I had even been in control. These thoughts would usually result in me realizing I was trying to give myself an easy out. Passing responsibility onto the test. I Always ended up forcing myself to take responsibility for my actions. In my mind, at least.

She was always able to respect my wishes and stay away from the tests. I simply reminded her we didn't really understand them; we both knew they were powerful. "It's not a good idea to mess around with forces beyond our comprehension." This was always my final statement on the issue and always seemed to get her to drop it. Things changed when she got word Keith was being released from jail.

It was pretty surreal to see her entire outlook change in the heartbeat it took for her to absorb the news. She went from carefree and life loving to exactly how she was before Keith got arrested. Scared and insecure. Looking behind her every minute like she was being stalked by a serial killer. Maybe she felt like she was. I did my best to support her, but it was like the smog that had been lifted from her only a few weeks before had fallen back over her world.

After a couple days, I decided I needed to try something else to cheer her up. She asked me to go out for some tea, and I stopped and got some flowers to bring her to go with it. When I got back to the apartment, she was shaking.

"What's going on? Are you alright?"

She composed herself quickly and gave me a big hug. "I'm better now. Thank you for the flowers and the tea."

I kissed her on the forehead and gave her another hug. "It's going to be alright, Claire."

"How do you know?"

"The universe told me." I kissed her again on the cheek, and she seemed like she was feeling better. The rest of the night we both did our best to act normal. Whatever normal was, I guess. The next day after school, she told me she had something to do and she would be home in a little bit. I felt a bit nervous, but I wasn't about to tell her she couldn't do anything. I also wasn't going to interrogate her as to what it was she had to do.

When she came home with a brown paper bag, I knew I had to at least ask. I didn't want to be anything like Keith, but I couldn't help feeling suspicious. When she pulled out the gun she purchased, it made me wish I had asked sooner. After my experience as a young journalist, I had no interest in having one in the house. But I didn't want to argue, and I reminded myself she was feeling unsafe. With some hesitation, I agreed she could keep it in the drawer next to her side of the bed. I didn't need to ask her anything about it; I could tell it was a magnum.

CHAPTER SEVEN

I AWOKE TO THE sound of a loud banging echoing through the apartment. I jolted out of bed to investigate. My heart was racing. I grabbed the nearest thing I could find, a statue of Buddha. I clenched it tightly by the neck and creeped into the living room. It didn't take long before I confirmed the sound was coming from the front door. It swung open with force as the intruder kicked it one last time.

I didn't need to be a detective to know it was Keith. I had never met him before; he didn't look like I pictured him at all. He was wearing a T-shirt with an 80s hair band on it. He was pretty tiny, and he had a gross little mustache and greasy hair. He had fire in his eyes. I lifted the statue above my head; my knuckles were white from my grip.

I took a swing, and he deflected it. The statue smashed off the wall and Buddha's head broke free, landing on the floor a few feet away. It was clear this guy was on a mission, and it was clear he was pretty intoxicated. He swung at me and connected with my chin. I fell to the ground, and before I could even process what was going on, he was on top of me.

"You motherfucker! You think you can steal my woman? You're going to die!" He was spitting as he screamed at me; I could feel the mist on my face.

I did everything I could to push him back, but he seemed to have some kind of super strength. I managed to push his head back enough it distracted him. Imagine my surprise when it exploded.

I heard the shot and saw the carnage at the exact same time. In a single moment, I watched the back of his head turn into fragments and splash all over the front door and the wall of my apartment. His eyes stared at me for a moment before he fell sideways. That stare stood out to me. He had a well-placed hole just under his left eye, a trickle of blood dripping onto my face.

I backed away, using my hands and my feet, as far as I could get from the body. My ears were ringing from the sound. I looked over to see Claire still holding the revolver. I sprang to my feet and started going in her direction. Her gaze was still fixed on Keith, but she was speaking to me as I drew near. "Don't, don't, don't, this will hurt someone."

I froze in my tracks. "What did you just say?"

She looked at me with some confusion and a bit of shock. "What?"

"What you just said... that was the last thing Budd Dwyer said before he blew his head off."

She wore a look of disbelief. She lowered the weapon and stared at Keith before looking back at me. "I just shot my ex-boyfriend in our living room and you're talking about Budd Dwyer?"

"Sorry." I tried to compose myself. I scrambled to my feet, then took a step toward the lifeless man on my floor. "Is he... dead?"

"I would fucking say so! Usually splattered brains is pretty fatal."

The aftermath was a bit surreal. I wish I could say I had never seen that kind of scene before, but obviously I had. I tried to think. "Okay, is the gun legal?"

"Of course it's legal." She still looked to be in a state of shock.

"Okay, then it's self defense. He broke in here with intent to harm us." I paused for a minute. "How did he know where I live?"

Claire shook her head to try to gain her composure. "You're right. He broke in here, we can just call the cops."

She seemed to be avoiding my question, but I decided to let it slide considering the circumstances. "I'll call them."

I picked up the phone and dialed 911. I explained the situation, and before we knew it, the light of various emergency response vehicles illuminated the street. I looked over to see Claire staring at the broken Buddha head that still rested on the carpet. I had a realization. "You used those cards again, didn't you?"

Before she could answer, the police came barging through the door. The paramedics followed close behind. We were taken to the station and questioned separately as they examined the crime scene. It was a bit stressful, but I didn't have anything to lie about. That had been the first time I had even met the guy, and he was breaking into my apartment to kill me. Kill us. I wasn't really sure.

It took several hours, but eventually we were both released without charges. They even let her keep the gun. I could see the tip of the handle poking out of her purse as we walked home. "Can we get rid of that thing now, please?"

She looked at me with some frustration. "You realize what I've been through tonight, right? Can we talk about this later?"

I nodded. I didn't want to pick a fight, but I also felt I deserved some answers. "How did he know where you were?"

"I called my mother to tell her he was getting out. She must have told him."

"Why would she do that?"

"She doesn't see the truth. Any time I've gone to her to try and get some respite, she always convinces me to go back home like a loyal wife."

"You weren't married, were you?"

She shrugged. "Technically, I guess."

"Technically? I don't think it's really a gray issue."

"We got married at City Hall. Nothing fancy. I was young and naïve and I don't like to talk about it."

I could feel tension in my stomach. Being married was a huge deal, but the guy was dead and I felt compelled to know about the test. I paused for a minute. "Did you give yourself another reading?"

"Why would you ask me that?" She was clearly defensive, which told me my intuition was probably accurate.

I didn't want to tell her I had killed someone on my second reading as well. Despite the fact she had just blown a guy's head off in front of me, I didn't necessarily trust it wouldn't cause her to panic. "A hunch."

I didn't want to press the issue too hard, even though my instincts were firmly pointing to the fact she had gone behind my back and used the cards. She adamantly denied touching the Rorschach since the reading I had given her. I tried to believe her, but I had a nagging feeling I couldn't shake.

By the time we got home it was nearly dawn. When I opened the front door to see all the blood still blanketing the carpet, I nearly retched. We tried to go to bed, but I couldn't sleep. I felt too shaken up. I decided I was going to go to school. I asked Claire if she wanted to join me, get her mind off of things and get out of the apartment. She wanted to stay home. I couldn't blame her.

It took all I had to make it through the day. Visions of Keith's face exploding inches away from mine were hard to ignore. I knew Claire was still shaken as well, but in the back of my mind, I hoped the blood would be cleaned off the floor by the time I got home. It wasn't. I could already smell death in the living room as it began to morph from a liquid to a gelatinous mass. I tried to scrub the carpet and pick up some of the bits of skull, but I didn't get a lot accomplished before I had to stop. I wondered where Claire was; I found her still in bed.

"Hey, Claire. You awake?"

"Hmph."

I crawled into bed beside her and draped my arm over her shoulders. I gave a squeeze. "It's going to be alright."

She rolled over and gave me a kiss. "Fuck him." She smiled as though the situation had never even happened. I was exhausted from being up most of the night and then being at school. I didn't even realize I had fallen asleep until the alarm went off the next morning to get me up for school. I sat up and rubbed my eyes. "C'mon, Claire. School time."

She rolled over and squinted. "I'm not going back yet. You have a good day."

"You sure?" I didn't want to press the issue since she did just have a traumatic episode, but I knew how important school was to her.

"Yeah, see you soon."

I kissed her and got dressed. By the time I got home, she was still in bed. I knew depression could cause long bouts of sleep, so I decided to just let her rest. I tried to clean up more of the living room. It was getting progressively more difficult as the smell of stale blood got stronger.

This turned into my new routine for a few days in a row. Going to school alone, and coming home and scrubbing until my arms felt like they were going to fall off. I would scour the place looking for spatter or chunks of flesh that were still hiding in the nooks and crannies. I started trying to put a bit more pressure on her to get back to the land of the living. "It's been days, Claire. Have you got out of bed at all?"

She rolled over. "Here and there. Don't worry, Lucas. I just need a few more days. Next week I'll go back for sure."

"You know I've been cleaning up bits of brains and skull all week. I know this is hard Claire, but a little help would be nice."

She rolled back over.

That weekend I tried to get her up and moving. She did have a few hours during the day where she came out and watched some TV with me, but she didn't seem to want to leave the apartment. We worked a little on the floor, but it was more time consuming than you may think. Maybe you would. I waited until Sunday to ask her again about going back to school the next day. She reassured me once again it would happen soon, but she still wasn't quite ready.

When Monday morning came, I didn't even bother trying to get her up. I still loved Claire, but I was getting frustrated. Keith was an asshole. It seemed like she had forgotten about all the beatings and the fear. All the time she felt like a hostage. It also seemed like she forgot the guy was on top of me when she blasted him. I know everyone handles things in their own way, but I was disappointed that I continued with life when she didn't seem to be able to.

School was pretty normal that day, up until my third class. Professor Mash was giving a lecture on the chemistry of the brain. Everything seemed ordinary until he began to choke on his words. Initially people thought he was kidding or performing some kind of ruse, but after he started foaming at the mouth, the reality set in.

Some students rushed to the front to try to help him, while others fled the room to call for help. It was a very theatrical death. It was unclear what was causing it, but he couldn't get any air and couldn't speak. He was flailing and bashing his hands off the desk. One student gave him the Heimlich maneuver, but it didn't do any good.

It was strange for me. I didn't move from my seat. Death seemed to be a regular part of my life at that point, and it didn't look much different to me than it would have if it had been on television. If I had to guess, it probably took him at least four minutes to die. It looked painful and frustrating. I found myself wondering how difficult it would be to become so desperate for something we all take for granted. Oxygen.

Paramedics arrived and tried to save him, but it was too late. Nearly the entire class had left or was trying to be helpful. I looked over at a girl named Marsha. She was doing the same thing I was—sitting there, watching. She had a different expression on her face; she looked content. She was friends with Claire. My suspicions quickly mounted about the inkblots. I couldn't quite place how, but I felt like they had been involved in what I just witnessed. I took my eyes off Marsha when she caught me staring at her.

My entire walk home that day I was fixated on questions. Had Claire been giving tests to other people while I was at school? Had she done a second test on herself? Dead bodies were not typically that abundant. Why Professor Mash? So many questions. I knew I had to confront Claire.

When I got home, the blood was still clearly visible on the carpet. I had spent so much time trying to get rid of it, but you could barely tell. The smell was starting to take over the apartment. Looking at it was like some sort of sign for me. I needed it gone. It also gave me something to do instead of talk to Claire about the day's events. I spent hours on my hands and knees, scrubbing. I used cleaners and bleach. By the time I was done it was mostly gone, but the carpet was still a different color. I was done with it. Off to bed and try not to wake Claire.

CHAPTER EIGHT

WHEN I WOKE UP, I did my best not to disturb Claire. She looked so peaceful when she slept. I was struggling a lot with my thoughts that morning. On a regular day, there was no doubt in my mind she was the right person for me. I sat and had my coffee. It was the first time I found myself asking if she really was she the right person, or if she was just the next step in my life. It was a strange thought, and completely foreign to me. On one hand, I believed she was my soulmate. On the other hand, I was feeling like she was being dishonest and had a lot more going on than she would admit.

I thought about the conversation I wanted to have. I would confront her about the tests, and she would continue to deny it. Even if she wanted to come clean, she was in pretty deep. I already felt enough stress that the idea of an argument wasn't very appealing. An argument I knew I couldn't win and would only intensify my growing feelings of mistrust.

I went to the bedroom door. "Claire? Coming to school today?"

She sat up. "What time is it?"

"Time to go. You coming?"

"Tomorrow." She curled back up and pulled the blanket over her head.

I could feel a strong emotion course through me. I made my way into the kitchen and opened the drawer. The three papers and the inkwell stared back at me. I scooped them up and put them in my bag. If she wasn't using them, she wouldn't even notice they were gone. Right?

I made my way to school and took my normal seat in class. Each day I would look beside me and wish to see Claire. Only phantoms. The lecture started as normal, and I tried my best to concentrate. It was about halfway through when the door opened.

I looked up and smiled when she walked in. Nobody else seemed to notice as late arrivals were par for the course. I kept my eyes on her and felt a sense of relief. Things were going to go back to normal. She was finally over the grieving of her dead husband, the husband she shot in the face in our apartment. I shook my head.

She sat down beside me.

"You came." I smiled.

"Where are they?"

I felt my stomach sink. "Where are what?"

She had fire in her eyes. It wasn't her. "You know damn well what I'm talking about. The Rorschach tests. Where are they?"

It dawned on me that as soon as I was leaving in the morning, she was getting out of bed and doing something with those tests. She wasn't depressed, wasn't sleeping all day and all night like she allowed me to believe. I felt an anger consume me and had to consciously keep my voice down to avoid attracting attention. "I don't know, you said you weren't using them."

"Where are they, Lucas?" Her voice was loud enough that the professor stopped speaking. I could feel all the eyes in the room fixed in my direction.

"Am I bothering the two of you?" The professor didn't try to hide his annoyance.

Claire looked at me with daggers. "See you at home." She got up and left the class without apologizing for the interruption.

I sank in my chair. I could feel my face was red, and I assumed the people near me could feel the heat radiating off of my cheeks. Soon enough, the class went back to normal. I couldn't focus; I had never seen Claire act like that before. I didn't know what to do, and the only guidance I had was at the bottom of my bag.

Once class ended, I decided to skip the rest of the day. It was something I didn't often do, but I was worried I may not get another opportunity. I left the school and headed to the park. There was a slow stream that flowed through it, and I came upon a quiet spot where I wouldn't be disturbed. I sat in the grass and watched the water for a bit. I loved water. It was a symbol to me that things always had to move forward.

Everywhere along the stream where something had gotten stuck, it was stagnate, filled with algae and not pleasant to look at. The running water was clean and clear. It had direction and purpose even if it didn't know where it was going. At least it was going. Maybe that's where the term "go with the flow" came from.

I opened up my bag and pulled out the inkwell, followed by the three sheets of blotter paper. I had never attempted the test in that type of environment before and was a little worried about wind and moisture, but at that point I didn't really care. Part of me wanted to throw it all in the stream and let it go wherever it ended up. I blamed the Rorschach for Claire's behavior. I blamed it for at least two deaths. Maybe it was just easier than taking accountability. Blame was always easier.

I used a button from my bag to prick my finger. It was enough that I could squeeze the three drops out I needed for the test. I dripped the ink onto the paper, and just as before, images appeared.

The first image was the gun Claire used to kill Keith. I hated that thing, and I wanted it out of my apartment. The next looked to be a wet floor sign, a standard plastic sign with a picture of a guy slipping and falling that people put down after they mopped. I was a bit confused about that one. I glanced to the third and final page, and it was marked with two X's. Cryptic.

I remember feeling a bit disappointed. I wasn't entirely sure what I was expecting to see, but I was thinking things would be a bit clearer. I put everything back in my bag and watched the water for another hour or so. I was fascinated by it and could feel my body getting more relaxed.

Inevitably I had to get back to reality and return to my apartment. I had no idea what state Claire was going to be in, and I wasn't sure how to address the situation at all. I took a deep breath and stood up from the bank of the stream, and slowly walked in the direction of home. I tried to understand how something went from so perfect to something that was making me so anxious in such a short period of time.

When I finally got back, I paused in front of the apartment door. It had been repaired to an extent, but there were still obvious indicators it had recently been kicked in. I had a flashback to Keith—the look on his face when he broke in and the life leaving his eyes as the bullet passed through his head. I took another deep breath and opened the door.

Claire was sitting on the couch, and she was alone. It looked like she had been crying. I wasn't sure what direction to go, so I decided to see what she said first.

"Hey."

"Hey."

"Sorry about today, I freaked out a little. You're right, I lied. I have been using the tests."

My first impression was she was being sincere. This was a relief to me because I knew I could talk to Claire. I wasn't sure how I could communicate with whatever I saw in class. I sat down next to her. "Why didn't you tell me?"

Tears formed in her eyes. "Because people trust me with their secrets, and I didn't want you overreacting or getting rid of them."

"I don't understand. What secrets?"

"First off, I did use it when I found out Keith was getting out of jail. I didn't know what else to do, and I knew you were super reluctant to use them twice. Even though you never really gave me a good answer as to why."

"What did you see?"

"Everything. I saw a phone, which turned out to be me calling my mom and telling her where I was. Then I saw a gun, and I went and bought one. Lastly, I saw a decapitated Buddha head. We both know where that fits in."

"Why didn't you tell me?"

"Why wouldn't you tell me that you killed that guy at Devil's Canyon. Chad?"

I felt my heart in my throat. "What? Who told you that?"

"Since I've started using these tests, my intuition feels like it's amplified, like I have some kind of spirit guide or something. I can't explain it, but my curiosity about you not wanting to do another test wouldn't get out of my head. I did some research at the library, going through some old newspapers. They called it an accident, but somehow I know it wasn't. Just like Keith wasn't."

Part of me was relieved. All the things I had started feeling after the test Claire was experiencing too. I wasn't crazy. It also felt good that I didn't have to keep that horrible secret anymore. "Why didn't you just talk to me about it?"

"Probably the same reason you didn't want to talk to me about that Chad guy. Nobody wants to admit to killing someone. But I bet that guy deserved it, right? He was doing something unforgivable?"

"Why would you say that?" I started to shiver.

"That professor that croaked in class, he was poisoned. My friend Marsha came to me about him before I had even met you. She made a mistake early in the year, but when she tried to break it off he blackmailed her. He was basically forcing her to sleep with him under the threat of ruining her potential career. When you showed me the cards, I thought I could use them to help her the way you helped me."

"One reading and she killed him?"

"No. The first reading came true, just like mine, and probably just like yours. It was easy to understand, and it really helped her. As soon as she found herself in trouble again, she was desperate for another. That's the one that killed him."

"You don't see anything wrong with this whole situation?" I knew in my heart I had no remorse for killing Chad. I also knew Claire had no remorse for killing Keith. Did that really make it alright?

She shrugged. "So far it only seems to kill bad people. Maybe it's a good thing."

"A vigilante Rorschach test?"

She shrugged. "You have a better explanation? Can I have it back, please?"

"Why?"

"I promised my friend Tasha that I would do one for her. She came over in tears today after you left, and I feel obligated. Last one, I promise. I'll never do it behind your back again, deal?"

I thought for a moment. I was glad to see the Claire I knew in a rational state and willing to talk. At that point, I was wishing I hadn't done the third test on myself before arriving. The gun. I needed to get rid of it before I ended up using it to hurt someone. "I'll trade you for the gun. You give me the gun so I can take it back, I'll leave the tests on my way out."

She nodded. "That's fair. I know you hate having it here." She stood from the couch and disappeared into the bedroom, returning momentarily with the magnum in her hand. She held it out by the handle. "Just take it back to the gun shop on third. It's called Sluggies. You won't need a receipt, just give Louie my name."

I accepted the weapon and slid it into the waistband of my pants. I leaned in and kissed her. "Thank you, Claire." I left the ink and the three papers on the table before I headed out to return the gun.

CHAPTER NINE

I FELT A STRANGE combination of nervous and safe as I walked down the street with a handgun. To be honest, I never thought the day would come after my experience as a young journalist, but there I was. Sluggies was only about a ten minute walk from the apartment, and I took long strides to try to get there even faster. When I found myself standing outside the door, I paused. I pulled the gun out to see if it was loaded.

In an instant, I had a flashback to the ink test—the image of the revolver halfway out of my pocket matched the vision I saw on the blotter paper. My heart began to race, and I quickly jammed the gun back out of sight. I took a deep breath and opened the door to the shop.

"Good afternoon, sir." The shopkeeper looked like a gun guy. He had a mullet and a handlebar mustache. He wore a trucker hat with a worn logo I didn't recognize. I took a few steps toward him and felt something touch my shin. I looked down to see a wet floor sign. It was again the same vision that had shown itself in the ink. My heart sped even faster. I wanted nothing more than to get rid of that gun and get home before anything bad happened.

I approached the counter. "Uhm, yes, are you Louie? I would like to return this gun. My girlfriend bought it and we don't want it anymore." I pulled out the revolver and placed it on the counter. I noticed the ends of the bullets, visible in the chamber at a glance. I hoped it wouldn't be perceived as any kind of a threat.

The man sniffled a little, kind of that mucus moving sound more than the runny nose sound. His demeanor changed from friendly to challenging. "What's the matter with it?"

I shrugged. "It kills people."

"Guns don't kill people. People kill people."

"Right, well, I'm sure it's still capable of killing people. She said I could just give you her name and you would take it back."

"Nope. Need a receipt."

I patted my pockets. "I don't think I have the receipt."

"Did you look in your vagina?"

"Pardon me?"

He scowled at me. "What kind of man don't want no gun?" He chuckled. "No matter. You come back with the receipt, and I'll sell it to someone who can use it."

I shook my head. I really had no words for that man. I took the gun off the counter and slid it into my pocket. I wanted to ask how to empty the bullets, but I already felt enough judgment. I made my way back toward the front door. I was about four steps away when I saw two men rushing toward me. They were wearing ski masks.

The door flew open and the men barged in with guns drawn. "Nobody fucking move!" One of them pointed their gun at my face. "Get on the fucking ground!"

The second man approached the counter and pointed his gun at the shopkeeper. "Give me the fucking money!"

He had a look of arrogance on his face. "Oh, I've been waiting for someone like you." He ducked down, and the masked man fired a shot that didn't connect. Louie emerged with a large shotgun and aimed it, pulling the trigger at the same time. The shot went through the robber's shoulder and he fell to the ground. This triggered shots from all three men, back and forth.

I watched in horror, knowing someone was going to die. Without much thought, I pulled the gun from my pocket and aimed it at the man who ordered me to the ground. I squeezed the trigger and hit him in the side of the head. Blood spattered all over the wall, and he dropped to the ground.

The other man turned to face me with his gun raised. I fired another shot that hit him in the chest. At the same time, a shotgun blast took his head clean off. It was the most gruesome thing I had ever seen in real life, like something out of a movie. His body jolted backward from my round, then forward from Louie's. Blood coated the room in both directions, and I could feel the warmth of it on my face.

The lifeless body fell forward, and the impact caused another splash of body fluids to paint the floor. Like a water balloon exploding right in front of me. I looked up at the clerk, who was still pointing the shotgun. I slid my gun across the floor and put my hands in the air.

"Don't worry boy, 'aint gonna kill you."

Once the initial shock wore off and I knew I was safe, I got back to my feet. Looking at the scene, I struggled to believe I was responsible. The shopkeeper placed his shotgun over his shoulder and smiled. "Maybe you 'aint such a pussy after all."

I looked at him a bit dumbfounded. I assumed that would be the closest thing to a thank you that I would get. He meandered back behind the counter and picked up the phone. "Yeah, Louie here over at Sluggies. Had a couple armed robbers that you'll have to come clean up." He hung up the phone. "Cops are comin'. They'll want to talk to you. Once they're gone, I'll give you a refund on that gun."

I nodded. "Thanks. This sort of thing happen a lot?"

He shrugged as he reached under the counter. He pulled out a marker and made his way toward the front window. He pulled down a small whiteboard and showed it to me. "This is how I warn these fucker's to stay away from here." He smiled, showing the few teeth he still had left. The board had about seven Xs on it, people he had killed that tried to rob him.

As I watched him with the marker, the Rorschach flooded my mind. He drew two large Xs on the board with the others. It was the same ones I saw in the ink. In one sense, I felt some relief, but in another I was creeped out. I wondered if my day would have been the same if I had never tried the third test on myself. Did it predict the future, or did it create the future? There was no way of knowing.

It didn't take long for emergency crews to respond. It took even less time for them to determine both of the robbers were dead. The police started taking pictures, and I gave my statement right there in the store. It seemed like they were pretty good with writing it all off as self defense. Which it was. Right?

Once the police had taken all the pictures they needed, they called the meat wagon to have the bodies removed. I had never heard anyone call it that before, but after hearing the terminology used by the police, it was now the first thing that came to mind. I was told I was free to leave. Louie kept to his word and looked up Claire's name in his records to find the purchase history on the magnum. He seemed more than happy to take it back. I figured it was probably worth more to some of those people once it had been broken in with a couple bodies.

As I was leaving, he called out to me. "You ever change your mind about a gun, you come see me."

I gave him a slight wave. "I will, Louie. Take care of yourself."

My world was once again feeling like a dream. It had been hard enough to battle the internal dialogue about Chad's death; now I had two more to add to the equation. I felt confident I would feel horrible if I had killed an innocent person, but these people didn't really fall into that category. The whole thing was pretty difficult to come to terms with. Was there such a thing as killing for the better good?

I decided to take the long way home. I needed some time to reflect. I had so many questions that I knew I could never answer. The one thing I could debate was what I should do next. I could tell Claire had a fascination with the tests, and I was fairly certain they were too powerful to mess with. I debated keeping them around for when I needed them, but they seemed to call to me and almost take away my free will.

On the other side of the coin, when would I ever come across something like the Rorschach again? The fact I stumbled into that fortune teller's building and got those cards must have been for a reason. It was like the universe trusted me with them. Maybe I was supposed to use them when they were needed. My thoughts felt like chaos in my head.

Those tests killed people. Killing people was never good, no matter who it was. I had to believe that. That would morph into thoughts of guilt or, rather, lack thereof. I struggled more with the moral questions than I ever did with guilt. I didn't care that Chad was dead. He would have killed me if I had given him the chance. The continuous loop. Was the Rorschach some kind of evil vigilante killing tool or something from the heart of the universe dishing out karma?

I walked around for a couple hours and struggled to come to any conclusions about how I felt. Ultimately, I decided getting rid of the tests would be the best course of action. Life was filled with enough drama. I didn't need to be special or have something nobody else had. I didn't care about power; I got into Social Services to help people. It was that simple.

Once my mind was made up, I headed back to the apartment and practiced what I would say to Claire. What it really came down to was that they were my cards. It was my ink. I had it all before I had even met her. If she had issues with me getting rid of it, maybe she wasn't the right girl for me. I tried to convince myself of that, but the closer I got to having to have the conversation, the more anxious I became.

I walked right past my apartment and did another loop around the block. I pictured all the things she might try to say to prevent me from getting rid of the tests and all the things I could say to counter it. I thought about walking away if she didn't accept my decision, but I loved her. Claire and I were connected on a level most people could never experience.

I sighed and did everything I could to clear my head. I was back at the door and couldn't completely understand why I felt so hesitant. I knew Claire was understanding, and I knew she was my partner. I decided I was probably just blowing things out of proportion. If I wanted to get rid of a few papers and a bottle of ink, surely she would support me.

I went inside. "Claire?"

No response.

I walked through the apartment and called her name a few more times. When she didn't answer, I figured she was probably sleeping. When I went into the bedroom and saw her belongings had all been cleared out, I didn't know what to think. Her bear was gone, and to me, that meant she wasn't planning on coming back.

I sat on the bed and put my head in my hands. I could feel the warmth of my tears on my fingers. I had so many questions. Then it dawned on me. Did she take it? I jumped up from the bed and ran into the kitchen. I opened the drawer, and my heart sank when I saw it was empty. Claire had bailed, and she took the Rorschach.

CHAPTER TEN

INITIALLY I WAS DEVASTATED about the loss of Claire. I felt betrayed and abandoned, and all the possibilities would race through my mind. I knew it came down to the ink tests. That was my ultimate conclusion, anyway. Sometimes I felt thankful they were out of my life, and other times I was angry and felt like I had been robbed. Regardless of how I was feeling, my circumstances remained the same. She was gone. The Rorschach was gone.

I got myself refocused on my education. I devoted all my time to studying and keeping my marks as high as I could. Over the course of the next few years, I was able to earn my master's degree in psychology. I spent another two years building my resume and honing my skills. I felt good about myself, and to be honest, I got pretty good at helping people.

There was a certain liberation in understanding your own mind. The stresses of the world would never cease to exist, but the more you understood yourself, the easier it was to analyze things and deal with the everyday challenges. Essentially, this was what I tried to help others understand, and for the most part, people were receptive. It was in the mid 90s that I opened my own practice and started building a clientele. I couldn't officially call myself a psychiatrist since I didn't have my PhD, but I still managed.

Things were going really well. I felt like a professional, and I was treated as such. All my thoughts about Claire and ink tests had faded into distant memories until something happened in late March. I had a man come in to talk; he was a regular client and I knew him well. He had a history he wasn't proud of, and he spent many years trying to learn how to forgive himself.

On this particular day, we had been talking for about ten minutes when he stopped mid sentence. I had a little bobble-head toy of Skeletor on my desk, and he fixed his eyes on it without blinking. "Have you always had that?"

Perplexed, I followed his eyes. "Skeletor? Myaah! He's always been there. Something wrong?"

He shook his head. "You would think I'm nuts. I think I'm nuts."

I was intrigued. "I don't label anyone like that. We all go a little mad sometimes. Why are you just noticing him now?"

"You know I've been trying to figure out how to deal with my past. At this point, I'll try just about anything to forgive myself for what I did to those kids. I heard about a place that had some kind of test that could show you the future."

An anxiety swept over me that I hadn't felt for years. It was all too familiar, and immediately I knew it had to be Claire. "So you did the test? What did you see?"

"I don't know. Probably nothing. It's like these three cards, right? She gets a few drops of your blood and mixes them with ink, and then pours a drop on each one. Visions appear. You probably think I'm bat-shit crazy."

"I believe you completely. Please, tell me what you saw."

He looked at me with skepticism; he clearly thought I was patronizing him. He had no idea how much I really did believe him. He sighed loudly. "Alright. First, I saw the face of a young girl. I swear to you I walked by the same girl after I parked my car to come here."

I nodded. "You said three cards?"

"Yeah, well, the second one was a skull with a hood." He pointed at Skeletor. "It looked exactly like that."

I poked at the toy to make the head bobble. "So two of them have already shown themselves to you? What was the third?"

"It was a stop sign."

I pondered the circumstances. "Is this the first time you've done this test?"

He nodded affirmatively.

"Alright, do me a favor? Make sure you come and see me before you agree to do another one."

He tilted his head. "What makes you think I'll do another one?"

"Well, it sounds like it's showing you things. That kind of power is hard to ignore. Next time you feel stuck, you may be drawn back to look for more answers. Call it a hunch. Call it a guess. Call it whatever you want, just promise me that you will come and meet with me before you do it again."

"Alright, sure, doctor."

We finished up our session and he left. I hated the idea the Rorschach was coming back into my life. I really had no proof; maybe it was a coincidence, but the feelings were undeniable. It had never been about the tests themselves, it had always been more about the overwhelming spiritual connection that followed. I started to feel it again.

Once he was gone, I approached my secretary, Sophia. "Hey, did Mr. Carlisle make a follow-up appointment?"

She smiled with her usual politeness. "Yes, Lucas." She looked down at her computer. "Two weeks from today."

"Thank you, Sophia."

I went back into my office and sat at my desk. I fixed my gaze on Skeletor. Despite the amount of time that had passed, I never truly felt like the tests were gone. It was like they were in hibernation. I realized that if those tests really were connected to me, then nobody could really steal them. I still didn't know what Claire had been up to, but I figured if she was using them as some sort of therapy, a lot of people could end up dead as a result.

This brought me back to my moral dilemma of who "deserves" to die. I had switched my focus to the other side. I wanted to help people learn how to live. All I could do was hope that two weeks later Mr. Carlisle would be back in my office with some sort of good news. Maybe he never saw the third image and decided it was a hoax. Maybe it helped him find closure somehow. Optimism was all I had, and it was soon shattered.

The next day, his picture was on the front of the newspaper. He died in a traffic accident. Not many details were given, but it did mention he collided with a stop sign. The story went on to say the police found "lewd images of minors" in his car and went on to search his apartment. All his dirty little secrets were brought to the light. On one hand, it made me realize he couldn't forgive himself because he hadn't stopped his behavior. But on the other hand, he had only done one test.

Myself, Claire, and Marsha all needed two tests before death was involved, and we all killed someone. How was it that with only one test this guy ended up roadkill and headline news? It was a mystery that would stay with me for another six months. Without him, I had no connection to Claire or the tests. All I could do was keep doing my best to help people and accept the knowledge she was out there operating somewhere.

I had a hard time getting it out of my head. One day between appointments, I had a chat with Sophia. "Have you heard anything about people taking some kind of test that shows the future?"

She giggled, her dark hair hanging in front of her face. "Like a gypsy or something? No. But a woman called to make an appointment to see you."

"A lot of people do that. Regular session?"

"No, she said it was a business proposition. She was very vague, and I told her you worked alone. She sounded pretty insistent and told me to at least let you know."

That feeling came back. "What was her name?"

"She said her name was Judith. She left her number, but I told her not to hold her breath. You can't just call a professional therapist and make cryptic offers with zero explanation and expect to be taken seriously, you know?"

"Sophia, I need that number."

She squinted a bit. "Seriously?" She reached down by her knees and moved some papers around in her waste basket. She pulled out a scrap paper with a name and number written on it. "I don't understand."

I took the paper from her and looked at it. "Judith." Who the hell was Judith? I tried my best to act normal. "I know. Normally you would be completely right and I wouldn't engage with this kind of thing. It's complicated, but I need to see what she has to say."

Sophia was clearly confused, but she was never one to argue with her boss. "No problem, Lucas. I'm sorry I threw it out. Do you want me to call her to schedule a meeting?"

I looked down at the number. "I'll take care of it. Thanks, Soph."

I ended up sitting with that phone number for two days. I must have picked up the receiver and dialed the first few numbers then hung up at least eight different times. Part of me was yelling at myself to stay away. I wish I could say I listened to that, but we both know I would be lying. The feelings of curiosity and unfinished business eventually got the better of me, and I called.

"Hello?"

"Judith?"

"Lucas. I knew you would call."

"Who are you?"

"That is irrelevant. You know the reason for my call?"

"Rorschach."

"Indeed. My employer feels that you could make a good team. She trusts you. She would like to meet with you in person, but she says she is concerned that you may still harbor some ill will toward her."

"Good fucking guess. What kind of team?"

"The details will only be discussed in person. I'm sure you understand. After all, you did call me."

That was a hard fact to debate. I could have easily ignored the whole thing. I wanted to, but I didn't. Claire knew I would call. It had been so long since she left me that I didn't realize the emotions that were still attached to her. Even the thought of her. It was the same emotions that consumed me when I first met her. Things I couldn't explain. I tried to remind myself she was just some girl, but deep down, I never allowed myself to actually believe that. "Okay."

"Splendid. She would like to meet you in the place where you first acquired the tests. Tomorrow evening after you close your office. She requests that you come alone."

I heard her hang up before I could ask any more questions. Why the hell would she want to meet me there? All the feelings I had relegated to the past were coming back full force. The world I had tried so hard to walk away from was surrounding me again, and I wasn't sure how to feel about it. It was overwhelming but also somehow felt right.

The whole thing was such a massive contradiction. Anything to do with those inkblots screamed of toxicity. Nothing good had ever come from those things, but I somehow felt they were my fate. I didn't even believe in fate. Fate removes free will and limits what we can do with our own lives. I had aspirations for myself, and I would never consider the option that I could only go as far as fate would allow.

So, if the fact I just said those tests were my fate, and I followed it by saying I didn't believe in fate, you have a pretty good understanding of where my head was at. What do you go with? Do you go with your thoughts or your beliefs? I thought I should stand up to Claire and never look back. That was logical. I believed I should see what was next for me and keep an open mind. That didn't make any sense, but it felt like I was being steered in that direction by forces greater than myself.

I met up with Claire.

CHAPTER ELEVEN

IT HAD BEEN YEARS since I had gone to that old building, yet somehow my feet seemed to know where to go. It was just like my first visit—I felt like I was being guided. As I walked, I couldn't help but wonder why Claire had chosen that specific location. I tried to remember if I had even told her where it was.

I wasn't entirely sure how to feel, either. Part of me was excited to see her, but another part of me wanted to punch her in the face and take back my tests. I knew I wouldn't do that, but I did practice all the things I was going to say to her when I confronted her. I was hurt, angry, and still feeling betrayed. I wondered what kind of answers she could possibly give me that could even come close to settling my queries.

Once I found myself in the seedier part of town, I knew I was getting close, but I also knew I had to keep an eye out. It wasn't exactly the safest place to be; people there could smell the money in your pocket. I left my wallet at home for that very reason, but still I kept eyes on my surroundings. The closer I got the more intense my feelings became. When I was within a block, I felt like I wanted to turn back and run, but I didn't.

Once the building was in sight, I could see a woman standing on the street near the front door. I squinted my eyes to see if it was Claire, but as I approached, it was clear it wasn't.

"Hello, Lucas."

"Who are you?" I looked her up and down. She wore a business suit and glasses. Her hair was cut to her chin and her eyes were a piercing blue. She looked like she didn't have a worry in the world despite being an obviously successful woman standing outside an abandoned building in crack town.

"I'm Judith, of course." She extended her hand. "I've heard a lot about you. It's nice to finally meet you."

I reluctantly reached out and shook her hand. "All good things, I hope." My heart was racing, and even just being back at that place put me on edge. "Where's Claire?"

Judith eyed the door. "She's inside. She just wanted me to meet you before the two of you spoke."

"Why?"

"We are partners, obviously. She wants to bring you in, and I have trust issues."

"Partners? In what?" I could feel myself getting angry, but for some reason, the fear and anxiety kept me polite. I wasn't sure what I was walking into.

She smiled. "She will explain everything. I'm sure you know what we do. Apparently none of our work would be possible if it hadn't been for you."

If there was any lingering doubt, it was gone at that moment. It wasn't about our relationship or her feeling guilty. It was about nothing more than those fucking Rorschach tests. "It wouldn't be possible if she hadn't abandoned me and stole from me?"

Judith tilted her head. "She was worried that you may be feeling that way." She opened the door and held it for me. "Go talk to her. She understands how you may be feeling and is willing to provide all the answers you need."

I paused for a moment and considered the invitation. Talking to Claire was the reason I had shown up, but my nerves were killing me. I glanced at the open door, then back at Judith, She still presented as a bit of an enigma. I slid past her and didn't break my gaze. My trust had to be earned.

I stepped inside and saw Claire sitting at the same table the gypsy occupied all those years before. We locked eyes, and I felt a strange sense of childlike infatuation, the same effect she had on me when we first met. She looked different but still somehow the same. Her hair had been cut short and was no longer blue. The hoop was out of her nose. She looked more like a businesswoman. Her eyes were the same—hazel gateways to her soul. A soul I trusted without reason.

"Thanks for coming, Lucas. I wasn't sure if you would."

Hearing her voice was like having a blanket of comfort draped over me, but I was still mad. "I wasn't sure I would either. You fucked me pretty hard, Claire."

She sighed. "I know it looks that way." She pointed to the chair across from her, the same chair I sat in after watching Budd Dwyer blow his head off. "Please, sit. Let's talk."

I was hesitant, but I pulled out the chair and sat. I wasn't sure how to feel, and I hoped that if nothing else, the conversation could bring me some clarity. I look at her. "Okay, so you probably know you left me with some questions. Care to explain what happened?"

She placed her hands on the desk. She noticed me looking at her finger to see if she was wearing a ring. "It wasn't another man. I never wanted to replace you."

I felt a sense of relief despite the fact I still wasn't able to forgive her. "So, what then?"

"We can dance around it all we want, but we both know the truth. The Rorschach has powers, and it was placed in our lives for a reason. We were placed in each other's lives for a reason. The whole thing is too powerful to be coincidence."

My first instinct was to lash out, but I didn't. Part of me wanted to tell her how stupid that sounded, but another part of me knew she was right. I put my head down and didn't speak.

"I knew that you were having doubts about it. You wanted to back out. You wanted to get rid of it, and I couldn't let you do that. Even if you had tried, it never would have let you."

"You're talking about those tests like they're a person, Claire."

"It's that exact attitude that made me leave. I see the potential in the tests, and they are bigger than anything that either of us could ever do on our own. I know you know it, but you don't want to believe it. I think you're ready now."

"Did the tests tell you that? What exactly have you been doing with them?"

"They did, in a way. I've been doing everything with them. I've been learning how to harness their power. I've been learning how they work."

"How many people have died from your experiments?"

"None that didn't deserve it."

"Who are you to say who 'deserves' to die?"

"This has always been where you need to open your mind. People like to take the high road. They like to think that when someone fucks them over that they will eventually get what they deserve. Karma will catch up to them. Someone will do something."

"What's wrong with that?"

"Nothing. But who is that someone? What is Karma? Who is going to step up for the little guy and actually follow through with that revenge?"

"You?"

"No. I just show people what they need to see. A power greater than myself takes care of the rest."

It was strange how the week before I had felt completely convinced Claire leaving my life had been the best thing that ever could have happened. It wasn't so much that she was convincing with her words, but more like she was sharing feelings that always lingered in the depths of my mind. I guess it was a lot easier to convince someone of something when you were tapping into unexplainable forces.

My logic was telling me she was as crazy as I would have been if I had given in to those tests. My instinct was telling me she was right. I knew they had power, and the fact I could never explain it caused me to retract. The part of me that wanted to prove my own sanity was all in the moment I saw her. The part of me that wanted to be a normal, functioning member of society reminded me how far I had come and how easily it could be destroyed by engaging in her ideas.

"Lucas, you're thinking too much. I can tell."

"I have to think, Claire. What do you want me to do?"

"You still have Judith's number?"

"Yeah."

"For now, just refer some clients to me."

"What, like the ones I think deserve to die?"

"Or kill."

"You're serious?"

She put her hands on her lap and straightened her posture. "Look, Lucas. I know that this his hard, I know it makes you question your morals, but have you ever thought about Chad?"

I was a bit surprised by the question. The truth was I had almost completely forgotten about that guy. "Not often, if I'm honest. Why?"

"Because you didn't do anything wrong. If he had been an innocent man, you would feel guilty. The fact that you don't should be enough proof for you to trust this."

I pondered the thought for a moment, but the facts were pretty obvious. "Chad was using his skills to kill people that he felt deserved to die. How is this any different? How is using this test to thin the herd any better than what he was doing?"

"He was a man. This test is the will of the universe. If either of us were doing this on our own accord for our own selfish reasons, the test would have dealt with us.

Instead, it used us as tools to remove people that were wasting space among good people."

"So, when Chad does it he deserves to die, but when we do it, we're acting on behalf of the universe?" My skepticism was building, but at the same time, I was starting to understand.

"Right. We didn't do anything. We were placed in situations where we had to act. Period. You never would have killed Chad if he wasn't trying to kill you. You aren't a bad person. You aren't a drunk driver. You were just figuring out his game, and he got scared that you were going to expose him."

I was starting to question myself. My morals. She had a point, but was it a rational point? Was it a way of thinking that could be adopted by a sane person? What was sanity? There were obviously a lot of things we didn't understand. Did enlightenment and madness go hand in hand? Were they one in the same? The need for clarity rushed over me, and without intention, I thought about taking another test for answers. As soon as the thought crossed my mind, I dismissed it.

"I know what you're thinking, Lucas. Don't fight it."

"What am I thinking, Claire?"

She pulled out a small blade and set it in front of her. When I just stared at it and offered no words, she proceeded to pull out the test. As soon as I saw it, a wave of energy consumed me. It had been so long, and I had done everything in my power to try to forget. There it was. She laid out the three pieces of blotter paper and set the inkwell on the table. It was so familiar and offered a reassurance I couldn't explain.

"I don't want to kill anyone, Claire."

"You won't. If people die, there will be no blood on your hands." She looked at the knife. "Well, maybe just a finger."

I tried to comprehend how I went from planning on cursing her out to considering letting her administer a test. It was a horrible idea. But why was I leaning toward doing it? Why was I extending my hand and allowing her to pierce my skin? Why was I now watching images appear in black ink?

A black dog.

A smile missing a tooth.

Two hands, engaged in a handshake.

CHAPTER TWELVE

T HE NEXT MORNING I felt off. Not sick or tired, just not
exactly like myself. I made my way into the office
and hoped that as the day progressed I would shake it.
I had a full schedule, and I was optimistic it would keep
my mind off Claire. I couldn't believe I let her give me
another test. I decided on that day I would prove to
myself the whole Rorschach thing was all in my head.
I wouldn't look for the signs, and I felt certain I wouldn't
see them. She was a nutcase and she was contagious.
Nothing more.

I arrived to find Sophia already there, as usual. She
looked sheepish. "Hey, Soph. You good?"

"Lucas, please don't be mad."

My anxiety gripped me in an instant. "Mad about
what?" I was afraid to know the answer.

"My husband got called in to work today, so nobody
was home to..." A tall black dog showed itself from under
her desk. "Nobody home to watch Zigmond."

I locked eyes with the animal. My entire plan of
avoiding images from the tests had been shattered the
moment I crossed the threshold of my own office. The

way the dog looked at me was identical to the image I saw in the ink the night before.

"Oh no, you are mad. He's a really nice guy, I promise."

I shook my head. "Oh, uhm, no, that's fine. I'm sure he is. I'm just concerned about allergies and such. Can you keep him in the back when clients are due to arrive?"

Sophia could clearly tell I was shaken, but she had no other explanation other than Zigmond. "I'm so sorry, I promise I won't bring him here again. He really doesn't have many behavioral issues. You won't even notice he's here."

I wanted to reassure her it wasn't a big deal, but I clearly couldn't tell her the truth. "No, it's fine, Soph. Just keep an eye on him and make sure he doesn't mess in the office. I'm not upset at you, I just have a lot on my mind." That was the closest thing to the truth she was going to get.

"Okay. Sorry again." She didn't seem confident but tried to change the subject. "You have a nine thirty with Joe, an eleven with Paul, and then Doug will be here after lunch, at one fifteen."

I nodded. "Thanks, Soph."

I headed into my office and sat at my desk. My mind was a mess. I had thirty minutes before my first appointment showed up, and I knew I needed to snap out of my delusions and get back to reality. The dog was a coincidence. I had to believe that. I felt like I was on the edge of something. I needed to step back into the world or plummet into the unknown. I wished I had never agreed to meet Claire.

Joe arrived for his appointment, and I was a bit surprised by how quickly I was able to slip back into normality and feel like my usual self. We had our discussion, and nothing out of the ordinary came up. Once he left, I felt better. My next appointment was very similar. Paul had been a client for a while, and our conversation was fairly typical.

When lunch came around, I stayed in the office instead of going out. I went to pet Sophia's dog to try to make her feel a bit more at ease about the whole situation. He seemed friendly, and I never saw him in the exact position of the inkblot again. I took comfort in petting his big, stupid ears, and for a few minutes, I felt like the whole thing with Claire was nothing more than her trying to drag me into her twisted fantasy world.

I was confident going into my last appointment. Doug was a new client; he had a court order to attend counseling. I was pretty good at getting people that had a bad perception of therapy to open their minds. I was almost excited. It was a combination of feeling liberated from the Rorschach and feeling confident in the skills I had built up over the years.

Doug came in and sat down across from me. He was middle aged and white. He wore glasses and had a well-kept appearance. My first impression was he was polite and relatively sophisticated.

"Welcome, Doug. What brings you here to see me today?"

"Not personal choice, I can tell you that much." His voice was raspier than I expected.

I looked down at my notes. "Says here that the court asked you to see me. Why do you think that is?"

He smirked. "Because they think I may harbor violent tendencies." He smiled wide. A tooth was missing from the front.

I ignored it. The image didn't match the test. Coincidence. "Why would they have that impression?" I looked back at my notes. "It says here you were convicted of assault and public intoxication."

He shrugged. "I was hitting on some guy's girlfriend and he tried to get in my way. Some people there felt that I was trying to drug her."

"Why would they think that?"

He stared out the window for a second. "Man, if those people only knew who I was. If they knew what I was capable of. They would never have messed with me."

I got a powerful feeling in the pit of my stomach but did my best to keep my composure. "Who are you, exactly?"

He smiled wide. It was the same image as the Rorschach. It was exact. "Well, now why would I go and tell you that?"

"We have rules about confidentiality here, Doug. You can't get to the root of your issues if you don't talk about them. You're only as sick as your secrets."

He laughed out loud. "Well, I must be pretty sick." He took a moment to choose his words. "Look, I'm not a dummy. I'm not saying I'm anybody, but can I ask you a question?"

My heart was racing. "Sure."

"Ever heard of Leonard Christopher?"

"Of course. He was the Frankford Slasher."

Doug smiled again, and again it was the same as the ink. "Was he?" He developed a look in his eye that showed he had demons. "Why'd they only get him on one? How did number nine happen when he was locked up?"

"Are you saying that you're the Frankford Slasher?"

"I'm not saying anything."

In an instant, everything I had been feeling the night before rushed over me. I had spent the entire day doing everything I could to prove to myself Claire was just jaded and crazy. There was no way what I was experiencing was any kind of self-fulfilling prophecy. I didn't want to see the images from the cards, but there they were.

I sat up straight in my chair. "You know, Doug, if you're not interested in this particular type of counseling, I could recommend you to a friend. The sessions are much faster, and you don't even need to talk if you don't want to."

He tilted his head and grinned. "Yeah, you're scared of me, right?"

"No. But I do have a duty to report. If we get into your past and I learn of anything that could be incriminating, I may need to include it in my report."

He laughed. "Yeah, sure. Okay, who would you be referring me to?"

I hesitated for a moment. What was I doing? I looked up at him and knew he had to answer for what he had done. If he was lying and he wasn't the real slasher, then surely no harm would come to him. I copied Judith's number onto one of my business cards and handed it to him. "This number is for a woman named Judith. Be sure and tell her that I sent you."

Doug took the card without breaking eye contact. He licked his lips. "A woman, eh? And the courts will be alright with this?"

I nodded. "Of course."

He kept his eyes on me and held the card between his fingers. "I'll think about it. We done here?"

I shrugged. "You're supposed to be here for an hour and a half, but if you agree to see my friend, I'll fudge the paperwork for today. I really think that you'll get something more out of seeing her."

I could tell he was skeptical. I imagined trust would be an issue for anyone who lied all the time. People tend to assume everyone thinks the same way as they do. He was silent for a moment before he answered. "Yeah, alright." He stood from his chair. "So we met for close to two hours today, right?"

I nodded. It was the first time in my career I would ever manipulate my paperwork. I had always prided myself on integrity. Somehow, I felt like I was testing the waters. Claire's waters. The waters of the universe. I couldn't say for sure, but I was compelled.

I watched him walk away. The Frankford Slasher killed nine women between 1985 and 1990. He sexually assaulted them before stabbing them multiple times and taking their lives. Doug was right, the guy they pinned it on was in jail while the last one had happened, and the case was totally circumstantial. If Doug was the real killer, he needed to be punished. I was in no position to make that call, but I found myself back in favor of the Rorschach, thinking it may be the perfect executioner.

I waited a few minutes before heading back out to the waiting room. I needed to find a way to make absolutely sure I wasn't losing my mind. I found Sophia still sitting at her desk. "Hey, Soph, we need to write down that the guy who just left was here for an hour and a half, okay?"

She grimaced a little. "But he wasn't."

"I know. I normally would never do this, but I told him he could leave. We don't want him back in jail for a decision I made, right?"

She nodded but still didn't look completely convinced. "I guess not."

A thought occurred to me while looking at my secretary. The last image on the test was two hands shaking. It was clear one belonged to a female. I extended my hand to Sophia. "Shake on it?"

She looked even more puzzled. I knew she still thought I was mad at her about the dog thing, and I may have used that slightly to my own advantage. She reached out and we shook hands. It became a little awkward when I held on a little longer than I should have. She may have found the whole thing creepy, but I needed to see the image. I needed to show the universe I still had control over my own destiny. Our hands were locked together for nearly a minute before I admitted defeat.

She stepped back a little. "Are you alright, Lucas?"

I nodded. "Yeah, sorry Soph. I think I zoned out there for a second. Why don't you take the rest of the day off? Take your friend Zigmond there for a walk or something?"

She kept her eyes on me. I had never seen her like that before; she looked almost afraid. "Okay. I'll do that."

I went back into my office and closed the door. With no more appointments that day, I had some time to think. Why was it taking longer for the images to reveal themselves? How did those things work? I knew Claire would be the only one that may be able to provide the answers. I reached for the phone and picked up the receiver. Before I had the third button pressed, I hung it back up. I needed to see what happened with Doug before I went any further.

CHAPTER THIRTEEN

OVER THE COURSE OF the next four days, everything was completely normal. I suppose "normal" was a relative term. The part of my brain that wanted to believe the whole thing with the tests was nonsense slowly started to take over. The issue was that when the other part of my brain emerged, I became almost obsessed. I asked myself why I hadn't seen the third image. The first series of images had shown up so quickly. Why hadn't I seen all three yet? Back to the other part of my brain. The reason was it was all bullshit.

On day four, I came into the office as usual after having my lunch. I checked in with Sophia. "Hey Soph, who am I seeing again?"

She rolled her eyes slightly. "I told you this morning, Lucas. You have a new client named Barbara at one fifteen."

I snapped my fingers. "Right. I knew that. Thanks, Soph." I made my way into my office and sat at my desk. I took a look at Barbara's file. Very generic, almost too generic. I figured I could use a simple client as the last one of the day.

It wasn't long before I heard Sophia through the intercom. "Barbara is here to see you."

I reached over and pushed the button. "Thanks, send her in."

In less than a minute, I heard my office door opening. I looked up expecting to see a new client; instead, I saw Claire. I scowled slightly. "Barbara?"

She smiled. I hated that her smile still made me feel warm. "In the flesh. Nice to meet you, Lucas." She closed the door and sat in the chair in front of me.

"Is this really necessary, Claire?"

"You tell me. Do you want to have a public association with me?"

"I never said I was going to have any association with you."

She smiled again. "I know, but as you are already aware, I have a knack for predicting things to come."

I scowled a bit; it felt like a dig. She stole my tests. Those were my tests. It should be my knack. "Did you get my referral?"

"Did the Rorschach guide you to that particular client?"

"You already know the answer to that, don't you?" I smirked a little.

"You smirk, but you know I actually do." She reached into her purse and pulled out part of a newspaper. "Seen this?"

I stared at it for a second before accepting it. I placed it on my desk and opened it; it was the obituaries. I scanned through and saw Doug. It said he died peacefully in his sleep. I looked up at Claire. "How did he die?"

"Is that really what you want to know? You know I can't answer that; the only one who could see the images on the cards was old Doug." She looked at me through her hazel eyes as though she was reading my mind. "You want to know if he was really the Frankford Slasher?"

I locked eyes with her. It wasn't the least bit awkward. "Yes. Was he?"

She smiled. "Of course he was. Even though it should have been headline news and it wasn't, you can still rest assured that you did the right thing."

"How do you know?"

"Please, Lucas. You don't find it strange that I knew that was your real question? You and I haven't spoken since you referred him. You think he told me? No. Judith gives me regular tests. I saw it in the cards."

The questions flooded my mind, but there was only one answer I really wanted. "Have you..."

"Killed anyone?" She tilted her head. "It's funny, Lucas. Every one of the clients I've served in the last couple years has had tragedy in their lives. They die, or someone around them dies." She smirked. "I've never been spoken to by the police. Most of my cases don't even become subject to investigations, and people's lives always seem to improve."

This really caught my attention. "So, no murder since Keith? Not a single drop of blood on your hands?"

She smirked. "No. I think that's the reason you had more than one."

"What?"

"Your skepticism. Once you put your full faith in the ink, it knows you truly believe. That's another reason that I'm here. You took the test again."

"And a man died."

"No, a brutal sociopath passed away in his sleep. No blood on my hands, or yours. You can try and fight this all you want, but I know you're starting to believe. At least enough that it showed you the way and didn't use you as the enforcer."

No matter how hard I tried to deny it, I knew she was right. I had always known the tests had power. I had always known Claire was not your average girl. As we spoke, I got lost in her eyes and she knew it. Even though I still hadn't seen the third image, I felt as though the test was complete. I made an impulsive decision. "Alright. I'll refer you clients, but I decide which ones."

She reached her hand out. I stared at it for a moment. Her skin was always so soft, and I was afraid of how it may feel to have physical contact with her. I reached out and we became one. On a business level, of course. As we were shaking hands, I looked down; I saw the third image. Somehow, I wasn't surprised.

She stood. "There is one last thing."

"Of course there is."

"You need to take the test again. You need to make sure you are sending the right people my way."

I sighed. "Alright. Why don't you come to my apartment later and we'll do another test."

She squinted slightly. "In other words, you feel like a blowjob may help mend your hurt feelings about me leaving?"

My eyes widened instinctively at the sexual content. "Whoa, I never said that." I sat back in my chair. She was still looking at me. "I wouldn't say no though." I smiled at her, probably the first genuine smile to grace my lips since she had left my life so suddenly all those years ago.

She made her way toward the door. "I'll be there at seven. See you later, Lucas."

"Close the door on your way out, Barbara."

As she left, she flipped me off. Even though I was still trying to be mad at her, I couldn't stop smiling. The same unexplainable feelings she evoked in me back in school were returning in full force. Maybe I was also happy I wasn't nuts. I felt clarity consuming me. The cards weren't a bad thing, and Claire wasn't a bad person. She did what she did so she could bring me back in when I was ready to accept the truth.

I took some time to catch up on my paperwork. I knew I couldn't make time go any faster, so I tried to make the best use of it. I left the office a little early and made my way back to my apartment. When I walked in the front door, I looked down at the throw rug I had placed there after Claire moved out. I thought about Keith's crime scene and all the time I had spent cleaning it up.

I looked at the drawer that used to house the Rorschach and the side of the bed that was once occupied by Claire. I was a bit conflicted, but I couldn't shake the excitement of having her over. I even debated making a nice dinner but decided against it. I tried to watch television for a bit, but my eyes kept migrating toward the clock.

At six forty-five, I began pacing. My heart was racing and I felt like a teenager waiting for his prom date. Every time I tried to remind myself of how much she had hurt me, the feelings were fleeting. When seven o'clock came, I started looking out the windows and through the peep hole on the door. At seven twenty, I heard a knock and almost threw up from the anticipation.

I straightened my shoulders and checked my breath before opening the door. She stood there, radiant as ever. I smiled wide. "Good evening, Barbara."

"It's a bit old now, Lucas." She winked at me. "You going to invite me in?"

I stepped out of the way to allow her to enter. "How's the night going?"

She shrugged. "Decent. You didn't make me any dinner?"

"Never even crossed my mind."

She looked around the room. "This place brings back a lot of memories." She looked down at the throw rug. "Probably the only way to hide those stains."

"Yeah, thanks for that."

She went over and sat on the couch. She assumed the same spot she once sat in every day. She looked at me with her haunting, alluring hazel eyes. "So, how have you been Lucas? Like, really?"

I sighed. I wanted to sit next to her, but I wasn't sure if I should. "Been doing well. After you left, I put all my focus into school, and then into work. What you saw earlier is pretty much the result of that."

"No lady friend?"

I could feel my cheeks turn a bit red. "No. Not since you." I cleared my throat. "How about you?"

"Ladies? Nah." She smirked. "No, nothing serious. I had a few encounters, but really it was work related."

"Work related? Hooker?" I didn't mean to say that.

She laughed. "My life has been devoted to these tests, Lucas. Here and there if I needed to get close to someone slimy, there was always a surefire way of doing so."

I nodded. I wasn't sure what to say, and I could tell she was picking up on it. The thought of her being with other men made me feel queasy. She placed her hand on the cushion beside her. "Why are you still standing over there? Come, sit. Are you afraid of me?"

"No, of course not." With the invitation on the table, I made my way over to the couch. I sat beside her and we locked eyes. I felt just as lost in her soul as I had when we first met. She leaned over and kissed me. I reciprocated. In that moment, it felt like she had never left. Her skin was just as soft as I remembered, and her lips tasted just as sweet.

Our chemistry hadn't faltered in the least. We made love on the couch just like we used to. We maneuvered each other's bodies with the same comfort and awareness as we had back then. That encounter reinforced in my head that Claire was the woman I was destined to be with. I tried not to think about everything that came along with her. I tried not to think about the Rorschach.

When we were finished we laid together naked for a while. We didn't turn on the television or even talk, we just enjoyed each other's company. Reacquainted with our united essence. It felt really good, and for the first time in a long time, I was happy. I would have done it all night if she hadn't brought up the inevitable.

"So, you're still cool to take another test? Get some instruction on who you're going to refer this week?"

I nodded. "Yeah. I'm not thrilled, but I'll do it for you."

She smiled. For a second, the thought crossed my mind—did she sleep with me for work? I decided not to ask. She stood up, and I followed her into the kitchen. We sat at the table. It was a strange feeling. I remembered showing her the tests in the same place. New information for her at the time that would later become an obsession. I wondered if I would have made different choices if I had the same knowledge at the time.

I took a deep breath and extended my hand. She had the three cards spread out in front of me, and the ink was ready to go. After a small cut, she dripped my blood into the vial and dripped it onto the paper. I held my breath for a moment before I fixed my eyes on the first card.

A swastika.

The second card. A teardrop.

Third card. A hand forming itself to look like a gun.

Chapter Fourteen

The next morning, I woke up alone. I had tried to convince Claire to spend the night, but she said she couldn't. We didn't really clarify anything about where we were as a couple, or if we were a couple at all. It weighed on my mind heavier than the fact I had done another test. She had a way of invading my thoughts and changing my priorities.

I headed into the office for another day. I chatted with Sophia for a few minutes and saw my first client. Nothing stood out. My second client was a different story. It was a man I had met with numerous times before, so I wasn't anticipating any surprises. His name was Lee. He wasn't exactly a model citizen, but he seemed to be trying to improve his way of thinking.

We were about forty minutes into our conversation when something completely normal happened. Lee had an itch. He slid his fingers up the sleeve of his T-shirt and scratched. It was only for a moment, but during this totally average ordeal, I saw it. It was a tattoo of a swastika.

I decided not to make any mention of it. I knew that whatever the reasons were that he had the ink, Lee was my next referral. "So, Lee, we've been making quite a bit of progress. Would you agree with that?"

"Absolutely. I'm really starting to feel like a better man. I never thought therapy could actually be helpful."

"There are many benefits. How would you feel about trying something a little different? Something that may help you with your journey and give you some clarity?"

He nodded, clearly intrigued. "What did you have in mind? You going to hypnotize me or something?"

"No. I actually have a colleague that practices some other methods. I would just refer you to her."

"What kind of other methods?"

"Nothing strange. A simple inkblot test to help light your path. She's quite good at helping people move in the right direction."

He shrugged. "Sounds a bit hokey, but if you say it's a good idea, I'll give it a shot."

I handed him a card. "Contact Judith, she'll set you up with an appointment."

He took the card and we finished our session. I went on with my day, expecting to hear from Claire. She never called. The rest of my sessions went well, and I didn't see any more images from the cards. After work, I spent my time pacing around my apartment and debating whether or not I should call Judith. It never even occurred to me until that night that I had no number for Claire. I must have picked up the phone seven times and hung it back up. I had a restless sleep and dreams about her.

The next day was very similar. All day at work I was expecting to see the second image, a tear drop. I knew in the back of my mind it would only reveal itself when the time was right, but the whole thing was making me anxious. Still no word from Claire. After a long, exhausting day I made it home. All that night I sat on the couch and watched the door, then the phone, then back to the door. Nothing.

The next day, I was struggling to focus. I had my two morning clients, and by the time lunch came around, I suspected the afternoon would be the same. I had a client named Stacey coming in. We had met before, and my notes indicated I had some difficulty getting a read on her. She seemed a bit theatric, but her problems were genuine.

She looked a bit worn, and she didn't hide the fact she was a drug user. She sat across from me and made it obvious she was having a difficult day. "I've been thinking of Samantha all day today; I can't get her out of my head."

I checked down at my notes. Samantha was the young daughter Stacey had lost the year before. The poor thing had drowned in the bathtub. "What kind of thoughts have you been having?"

"Just..." She started to cry. "Just remembering her and wondering how things would be if she were still here." Her tears continued, and in the briefest of moments, I saw the image from the ink. Stacey was my next referral.

With that in mind, I almost saw her differently, like a switch had been flipped in the same blink of an eye as I saw the image. Crocodile tears. She must have done something to that baby. "Do you want to talk about what happened to Samantha?"

She took a deep breath and wiped her eyes. We spent nearly thirty minutes going over what had happened to her daughter. It turned out that while Samantha was having a bath, the phone rang. By the time Stacey got back, just a minute later, Samantha had drowned.

It was strange listening to the details. I was always very empathetic and gave people the benefit of the doubt. After the picture revealed itself, I saw Stacey differently. I knew she had been on drugs and neglected her child. I saw through her façade of grieving mother. I knew her own selfish behavior had caused her daughter's early demise.

I gave all the appropriate answers, and my demeanor was professional. Once we were almost done with the session, I brought up the idea of trying something new.

"A what test?"

"Rorschach. Like the inkblots."

"I'm not sure how that would help, but if you recommend it, I'll give it a shot."

I handed her the card with Judith's number before she left my office with tears still in her eyes. Once she closed the door, I decided it was time for me to get some answers. I dialed the number myself.

"Hello?"

"Hey, Judith. It's Lucas. Can I speak to Claire?"

"She's not available. Can I help you with something?"

"I want to talk to her. I just sent my second referral of the week, and she hasn't reached out. Do you have her number?"

There was a pause. "I'm not permitted to give out that information."

"Judith, you know the deal. Claire won't care if you give me her number."

Another pause. "Lucas, look for the last image. Once you've exhausted the test, she will meet with you to perform another. I thought she was clear on that."

I thought about our time together on the couch. "She was far from clear on a few things; that's why I need to talk to her."

"Lucas, I have to go. Once you've established your third referral, she'll be in touch." She hung up the phone.

"Hello?" I slammed the receiver down with a bit more force than was necessary. Feelings of frustration were taking over. Why wouldn't she talk to me? Was she my girlfriend again? Had I made a huge mistake?

I tried to focus on my paperwork, but my mind was clouded. I left the office and tried to compose myself.

"You alright?" Sophia was packing up for the day.

"Fine. Thanks, Soph."

"What was that bang I heard?"

"It was a fly. Don't worry, I got it. See you tomorrow." I headed out before I said anything rude. I wasn't in the mood for small talk, even with my secretary. I made my way back to my apartment and tried to sort out my feelings. How was it I had the skills to help people get their lives on track, but I couldn't handle the emotions I got from dealing with Claire?

I did my best to kill the evening with television, but I couldn't focus. I must have formed my hand into the shape of a gun at least fifteen times to try to see the image. I wanted it to be over. Every single attempt was a failure. I wondered if my infatuation with Claire was detrimental or productive. I couldn't understand how my focus could swing so far on the pendulum so quickly and so often. These thoughts eventually wore out my brain, and at some point, I fell asleep.

When I went into the office the next day, I looked horrible. I felt just as bad and wanted more than anything to see the last image. I decided I was done with Claire and her games. I kept to myself all day. During my appointments, I struggled to stay focused. I even tried once to make the gun shape at a client to see if they would do it back. There was no way to force the images. I figured that out conclusively that day.

That night was almost a mirror image of the one before with the exception of me trying to force the last card. I was getting more frustrated and more confused the longer I didn't hear from Claire. I debated going to the liquor store and getting something to help me sleep but decided against it. Alcohol was never much of an allure for me. Sleep came naturally at some point, but that's about all I could remember.

The next day was the one I'll never forget. It was the day that changed everything for me. My second appointment was due to arrive. I was reading his file. I noticed on his chart he was only seventeen years old. When he came into my office, I would have guessed him to be around twelve. He had a baby face and curly blonde hair. His parents had set the appointment to try to get him to open up to someone.

"Hello, Travis. How are you today?"

"I don't want to be here." His voice was still high, a late bloomer perhaps.

"Okay, well since you are here, why don't you tell me a bit about yourself? We have an hour."

"Why would I want to talk to you? My parents made me come here."

"Why would they do that?"

"Because I hate everything. School is the worst, and so are you."

I nodded. "I understand why you would feel that way. I wouldn't want to talk to someone I was forced to see, either." I left a moment of silence. "The thing is, Travis, this isn't about them. They will never know what we talked about in here. It's confidential."

He smirked. "Oh yeah? Sometimes I wish I had a gun. I could shoot them all." He shaped his fingers; it was the third image.

I froze for a moment. There was no way I could send a child to Claire. He didn't deserve to die, and he wasn't about to kill anyone. He was clearly just misunderstood and depressed, likely due to his late development. The empathy I prided myself on returned, and the thoughts that had been driving me mad over the week subsided. I felt like myself again.

Over the course of the hour, I used every trick I had to get the kid to talk. It turned out he was being picked on at school and his parents were constantly fighting. Pretty typical of an adolescent's complaints. We talked about his goals for the future and how there was way more to life than just high school. He ended up getting pretty engaged.

By the time he left, I felt certain I had made some real progress. He even said he would see me soon. I felt accomplished and proud. I remembered in that moment why I had gotten into the field in the first place. I thought of Budd Dwyer. Frustrated, disappointed, and wanting to make a statement. Technically the real reason I had switched careers. The kid was different; he just needed a bit of guidance and encouragement.

My third appointment went equally well. I was on my game. All I had to do was keep Claire out of my mind, and I could appreciate everything I had worked so hard to build. I decided in that moment that if she ever did show up at my door again, she wouldn't be allowed in. My life had been so much better without her in it.

As I left the office that day, I had two thoughts that repeated themselves in my mind.

Fuck Claire.

Fuck the Rorschach.

Chapter Fifteen

T HE WEEKEND PASSED WITH its typical tedious hours of unentertaining television and monotonous time-killing tasks. It was the first time I had really been appreciative of that. With no Claire, there was no stress. It did get me thinking, though. The thought of having a woman in my life again was something I hadn't put a lot of energy into considering. I figured since Claire had shown me her true colors, maybe I would be able to move on.

Sunday night, the thoughts of dating snowballed into a realistic plan. I headed into work Monday morning feeling pretty good. I felt like a huge weight that had plagued me for a long time had been lifted off my shoulders. The weight of Claire. The feelings associated with her and the Rorschach. When I made it to the office, my secretary was already at her desk. "Hey, Soph, how was the weekend?"

"Good, Lucas, you?"

I nodded. "Boring. Do you happen to have any friends that you think I would get along with?"

She smiled. "Are you asking me to set you up on a date? That's so cute."

"It's not cute, Soph. I'm a grown man." I tried to keep a serious face, but I felt a little giddy at the prospect of meeting a new woman. It was exciting even though it hadn't even happened yet.

She smirked again. "I'll make a few calls. Here's your files for the day."

I smiled as I took the stack of folders. "I owe you one."

"You owe me more than one, Lucas."

For the rest of the day, I was in a great mood. Claire had been the only woman I had ever been with except for a couple girls back in high school. While I had clients, I was on the ball, and when I was in between, my focus was on the future. I once again doubted the whole concept of fate. The universe wasn't in control of my life, I was.

When I was leaving for the evening, I chatted with Sophia again. "Have a good night. Say hello to Zigmond for me."

She smiled. "Alright, since you remembered my dog's name, I'll hook you up with the hot one."

I blushed a little. "Oh yeah, I almost forgot."

"Sure you did."

"See you in the morning, Soph."

I left that night with more optimism than I had experienced for a while. I felt like I was finally closing a chapter of my life that had never really served me in the first place. When Claire wasn't around, I felt a sense of clarity that changed my entire perspective. I tried to keep in mind that if I did see her, she had more of an effect on me than anyone else I had ever met.

The release I was feeling made it a bit difficult to sleep, but when I finally did, I stayed that way and woke up feeling pretty well rested. I made my way into the office, and as usual, Sophia was already there. "Morning, Soph."

"Morning, Lucas." She reached in her drawer and pulled out the files for the day. "Here are your appointments."

I paused for a second before accepting them. I decided not to say anything, but I had been secretly hoping she would have a date set up for me. I took a few step toward my office.

"Aren't you going to ask about my friend?"

I froze in my tracks, and I could feel the grin overtaking my face. "Friend? You found someone?"

"Of course. Her name is Melody, and she wants to meet you after work for some drinks. Interested?"

"Melody? That's a nice name." I tried to pretend like I was pondering. "Sure, why not?"

Sophia rolled her eyes. "I already told her you would be there."

"You're the best, Soph."

"I know."

I went into my office and prepped for the day. My clients were all engaged, and I felt good about all my appointments. I found myself staring at the clock any time I was alone. I felt like a kid again. Even though I had never met Melody, or even knew what she looked like, I couldn't wait for my date. Eventually the time came for me to head home.

I stopped at Sophia's desk on my way out. "I really do appreciate you helping me out with this; it's a bit embarrassing."

"We all need a little help now and then. She'll be at Pablo's Bar and Grill at seven. She's the redhead with the nice rack."

I smiled. "I like her already." I looked down at myself. "What should I wear?"

"Not that. You're going on a date, not meeting a lawyer. Casual clothes. Do you even have any casual clothes?"

I thought for a moment. "Like what? T-shirts? Jeans?"

"Yeah, Lucas. That's what most normal people wear. You'll seem like a pretentious ass if you show up wearing a suit and tie."

I nodded. "Duly noted. Thanks Soph." I headed toward the door.

"I told her you were cool, so don't be a huge nerd, okay?"

I looked back before closing the door. "No promises. See you tomorrow."

I felt like I was floating as I made my way to my car. I tried to imagine what the girl would look like and what we would talk about. The one thing I knew for certain was there would be no conversations about ink, the universe, or seeing the future. Sometimes you just need to enjoy the little things.

When I got back to my apartment, I scoured my closet for something that wasn't business attire. I didn't have a lot. I managed to find a band shirt a friend had given me as a joke and I had never worn. I hoped it was a band, anyway. It said Butthole Surfers across the front. I didn't have any jeans, but I figured the shirt would balance with some black dress pants. I was ready to hit the town.

I made it to the restaurant by six thirty. I ordered a drink and kept an eye out for a redhead. I tried not to drink too quickly to calm my nerves because I knew it would hit me pretty hard, and I wasn't really a fan of the taste of alcohol. I sat there with my piña colada and tried not to look like the weirdo sitting by himself.

"Lucas?"

I looked up to see a gorgeous woman standing in front of me. For a moment I wasn't even sure how to answer her question. "Uhm, yes. Yes, that's me. You must be Melody?"

She smiled. "That's me." I could feel her eyes checking me out. "Nice shirt. Who was in my room last night?"

I felt awkward. "Uhm, I'm not sure."

She rolled her eyes. "You're a Surfers fan?" She sat down across from me. "Music is always a good way to get to know someone."

I had forgotten about my T-shirt. "Oh, yeah, totally. Now I get it." I had no idea what she was talking about.

"You hear that one that Gibby did with Ministry? Fucking killer."

I nodded. "I don't actually know that much about them. I just didn't have any other shirts to wear."

"I like an honest man. You going to get me a drink?"

She wore a nice dress that really showed off her contours. Her face was smooth, and her hair was half tied up in a messy bun. I could tell Melody knew a lot more about casual dressing than I did. "Sure, what would you like?"

She glanced at my drink. "Nothing girly like that. Just a beer, please."

I nodded. For some reason, I thought of the nutcase who owned the gun shop. Why are sensitive men labeled as girly? I wasn't about to let it ruin my evening. I went to the bar and ordered a beer. I asked to have a menu brought to the table and rejoined my date.

"So, Sophia tells me you're her boss? A shrink?"

"Technically I'm not a full-fledged shrink just yet. I need to go back and get my PhD before it's official. I see clients and we talk about their issues."

"So, you're a shrink?"

Even though her words could be perceived as slightly condescending, I found Melody interesting right away. She was beautiful, and I envied her attitude. I had spent so much time trying to learn how to be professional that somewhere along the line I forgot to learn how to enjoy myself. When the waiter came by to take our order, I got a burger and a beer.

The night flew by, and I had a genuinely good time. It was fun. I learned she worked as an accountant and had a small cat named Polly. She seemed interested in getting to know me, and never once did the topic of inkblots get brought up. It was relaxing, and she even smiled once when she caught me looking at her chest.

We were out until close to eleven, and I had consumed more beer than I ever had in a single evening. I paid for the night and we made our way to the parking lot.

"I had a wonderful time, Melody."

She smiled. "So did I, Lucas. You aren't planning on driving are you? You don't seem to handle alcohol very well."

"What do you mean?" I stumbled backward and nearly fell on my ass. "You want to come to my place?"

She steadied me with both hands. "I like to take things a bit slow and not take advantage of drunk people. I will give you a ride, though." She watched me struggle to keep my balance. "Actually, I insist."

I felt like the world was spinning, and I knew there was a definite possibility I would throw up at some point. "Okay. Will I see you again?"

"Sure. But first let's focus on getting you home." She put her arm around me, and I put mine around her. Mine may have been wandering a bit but she didn't say anything. She pointed to a black sedan. "That's me."

She helped me into the passenger seat, and I tried my best to give her directions to my apartment. I only drank five beers, but apparently that is a lot for someone who barely ever touched alcohol. I must have given her some wrong turns, and she started looking nervous. "This is where you live?"

I forced my eyes open and through my blurry vision, I could tell we were in the seedy part of town. Not only that, but we were right in front of the dilapidated building that once upon a time introduced me to a gypsy. And some tests. I felt my stomach sink, and I opened the door and threw up on the road.

"Holy shit, Lucas. You alright?"

I wiped my mouth and closed the door. "Yeah, sorry." The sight of the building sent chills up my spine. "This isn't where I live. I must have gotten confused." I pointed to the left. "Turn here, I'll show you."

"You sure you know where you're going?"

I nodded. The directions I gave after that were all spot on, and we finally pulled into my parking lot. She left her car idling near the front door. "You alright from here?"

I looked into her eyes; they were so pretty. "Maybe you could help me?"

She turned the ignition off and got out of the car. I opened my door and nearly tripped getting out.

"You didn't get any puke on my car, did you?"

I looked down and tried to focus, but the world wasn't the same. "I don't think so. If I did, I'm sorry."

She laughed a bit. "Man, I wish I could get that smashed off of five beers." She came over and looked at the passenger door before offering her arm. "Looks clean."

I nodded. I was about to take hold of her hand when I noticed something that changed my entire mood. There was a woman standing near the entrance of my building. It wasn't just a woman, it was Claire. I stood up straight and looked at Melody. "You know what? I think I'm okay to get in."

She could tell that something was different about me. "Are you sure?"

I nodded. "Yeah, I don't want to be creepy or anything. I had a great night with you and I don't want to ruin it. I'm good. Thanks for everything."

"Alright, if you say so. It was nice to meet you. You just barfed, so this is all you get." She leaned over and kissed me on the cheek.

In that moment, I forgot about Claire instantly. That giddy feeling swept over me, and a smile stretched across my face. "Thanks for the ride."

She smiled and reached into her purse. She pulled out a scrap of paper and wrote down her number. I took it and smiled; I figured I hadn't blown it completely. I watched her get back in her car and drive off. I was dizzy and tired and just stood there for a minute.

Claire waited patiently by the door.

CHAPTER SIXTEEN

I DID MY BEST to act normal as I stumbled my way to the entrance of the building. I kept my eyes fixed on the ground and decided I would just pretend I didn't see her. I thought it actually worked. I went in the front, then unlocked my apartment. I swung the door closed behind me, but instead of latching, it bounced back open. Claire was standing there with her foot in the threshold.

"Hey Lucas."

I wasn't sure if she saw me with Melody or if she would even care. My brain wasn't working properly, and I wished for nothing more at that moment than to be sober. "Hey, Claire."

She kept her foot in place. "Aren't you going to invite me in?"

My head was still spinning and my eyelids felt like they were equipped with ten pound weights. "I'm going to bed."

She forced her way past me and into my living room. "This won't take long, Lucas." She sat on my couch and patted the empty cushion next to her. "Come. Sit."

The alcohol freed my tongue. "I said I don't want to talk to you. You come over and sleep with me, and then you vanish again. You're fucking my head right up and I can't do it anymore."

She rolled her eyes. "That's what this is about? You're butt hurt that I avoided you after we had sex?"

"Not just that." She had a way of minimizing my feelings. It was my job to help people sort through their emotions, yet somehow I struggled with my own.

Her demeanor became very serious. "I don't care if you want to fuck other women or you want to fixate on me. The point here, Lucas, is that you broke the deal."

"What the hell are you talking about?"

"The third referral. The third image. I know you saw it."

I felt the air escaping my lungs. I was like a small child caught red handed stealing from his parents. "Claire, he was a fucking kid for Christ's sakes. He wasn't dangerous; the test was wrong. He just needed some guidance, like every teenager."

She realized I wasn't going to join her on the couch and stood. She reached into her purse. "Was his name Travis McTavish?"

"Let me guess, the fucking Rorschach told you that?"

She pulled out a newspaper. "No, the paper did." She handed it over to me.

I read the headline and as much of the article as I could focus on. It turned out that Travis had gone to school a couple days after our session and shot four other kids before turning the gun on himself. The feelings of guilt and confusion caused me to stumble and almost fall over. "What the fuck?"

"You swear a lot when you drink, did you know that? What did you have? Like three beers?"

I decided to ignore her question. "So what? If I sent him to you he would still be alive?"

"Probably not, but maybe he would have blown his head off alone in his room and not taken four other kids with him. You can't go playing God, Lucas."

"That's exactly what that fucking test is doing, Claire."

"That test *is* God, Lucas."

I shook my head. "I just want to go to bed. What do you want from me? Why did you come here?"

"You know what I want." She pulled the vial of ink from her purse.

"No fucking way."

She took a step closer to me. "You don't have a choice, Lucas. You've been chosen by the Rorschach. We both have."

"Claire, I've had a great night up to this point. I decided to move on from you. You've broken my heart and caused me so much confusion that I just can't do it anymore."

"We've been over this. You're confused because you know that the power is real. You know you have an obligation to the universe."

"Fuck the universe."

"Keep talking like that and the ink may get angry. If you don't believe it really has any powers, though, I guess that doesn't worry you."

I felt a wave of alertness and pseudo sobriety wash over me. One thing I couldn't debate was the strange things I had seen as a result of that test. I took a deep breath and tried to focus. "Okay, so what? I do the test and you just ignore me until you decide it's time to randomly show up uninvited at my apartment in the wee hours of the morning?"

She looked at her watch. "It's eleven-thirty."

"Really?"

"Yeah." She took another step closer, still holding the bottle. "If anything ever happens, we don't want any record that we were communicating, right? You've worked so hard for everything you have now, and I don't want your heroism putting that in jeopardy. I'll come every time I get the third referral. I'll make sure I get here early. Mind you, I waited for you for over an hour tonight."

I felt defeated. I kept switching my eyes from the bottle of ink to the hazel abyss that showed me her soul. I was drunk. I felt guilty. I caved. "Do it."

She took my hand and pulled a small knife from her pocket. She made a short slit across my fingertip and caught the three necessary drops of my life force in the small mouth of the bottle like a professional. "Let's go to the table."

I followed her like a lost puppy and watched as she spread out the cards and dripped the ink I knew would haunt me for the foreseeable future. The first image took shape. It was a briefcase. I focused as best I could as the second image formed. It was a cat.

When the third image appeared, I squinted. I couldn't tell what it was, it just looked like some sort of shapeless blob. I looked up at Claire. "That one doesn't look like anything."

"You'll see it when you need to." She stacked the cards and put them back in her purse, with the inkwell. "That wasn't so bad now, was it? By the way, who was the girl? Something serious?"

I wasn't sure how to answer. Part of me wanted to say it was very serious, but those eyes trapped me every time. "That was our first date."

She nodded. "She's cute. You better get some sleep, the streetlights are on."

She left as quickly as she came, closing the door behind her. I went into my room and face planted onto the bed, wishing the night had ended with Melody dropping me off.

I woke at my usual time, without my alarm clock. Apparently I had forgotten to set it the night before. I felt fairly normal with the exception of mounting anxiety in the pit of my stomach. What had I done? I tried not to think about it. I had to call a cab to take me to my car, which was a good enough distraction for at least part of my journey to work.

When I entered the office, Sophia was beaming. "Well? How was your date with Melody?"

I started smiling a bit, I couldn't help it. "You were right, she's very pretty."

"I said she was hot. You get lucky?"

"I drank a bit too much."

"Two beers?"

"Not you too. Have you spoken to her?"

"No, not yet. You going to see her again?"

"I hope so. I had a good time. I need something normal in my life."

"What does that mean? I'm normal."

I laughed. "Soph, you are far from normal. Do you have the appointments for today?"

She chuckled as she reached into her desk. "Yep, here you go." She handed me three folders.

"Thanks, Soph, have to prep. We'll chat later."

I went into my office and closed the door. I scanned the files for anything that may give me a hint as to who I was looking for. I was already in emotional turmoil after seeing Claire for half an hour. I was trying to focus on Melody and moving forward with my life, but I knew the images were going to show themselves sooner or later. I couldn't avoid it. I felt so stupid for taking that test again.

When my first client arrived, I tried to keep my mind on the task at hand. I couldn't help looking for signs, but she didn't have a briefcase. The conversation ended up going well, and before she left, she thanked me for my time. Another job well done.

My next client was a man named Rob. When he came in, I had a feeling right away he was image number one. He had a briefcase but wasn't dressed at all like a man that would carry one. I tried to remind myself I couldn't force the images. I had tried with the one of the hands shaking, the one that ended up with me making a deal with the devil. The universe. Whatever. Claire.

Before Rob sat down, he placed the case on my desk. There it was, the exact image from the ink. Before we even started talking I knew I had my guy. It was the first time I had to sit and give advice to someone I knew I was about to send to their death. I did my best. "What brings you here today, Mister Clark?"

"Well, doctor, I'm having a bit of a crisis. My mom recommended that I talk to someone. You know, moms."

"Right, well, I'm glad you're here. Though I'm technically not a doctor, I still hope I can help you with whatever is causing you stress."

"You aren't a doctor?"

"No, but I have a very good education and I'm good at what I do. Why don't you tell me what's been bothering you?"

He reached for his case but pulled his hand back before he got to it. "You people, you're all the same. I'm so sick of people. I hate society. How do you get a job like this without being a doctor and I can't even keep a gig as a forklift operator?"

"What happened? Were you let go?"

"That's a nice way of putting it. I was canned. Again. I can't keep a job, I can't get a date, and I'm thirty years old still living with my mother. Fuck this, I'm out of here."

As he began to stand, I put up my hand. "Hold on, Rob. Would you be interested in something that isn't the same as everything else?"

"I'm listening."

"I have a colleague that I think may be able to help you. Would you like the number?"

He picked up his case and extended his other hand. "If it'll get my mother off my back, I'll try it. Give me the number."

I pulled out a small paper and wrote down Judith's number. I handed it to him, and he left without another word. It was difficult to help someone who couldn't take accountability for their own actions; I just hoped Claire would have better luck getting through to him than I did.

With the appointment ending significantly early and nothing else until after lunch, I decided to call Melody to check in on how she was doing. I was a bit worried I had embarrassed myself the night before. I pulled her number out of my pocket and tried to call her. I got a busy signal.

I hung up the receiver and went out to see Sophia; she was on the phone. I could tell it wasn't business related by the things she was saying.

"Oh yeah? See, I guessed two..." She paused as she listened. "Really? Butthole Surfers?" She laughed. "So are you going to see him again?" Another pause. "That's great, I'm glad it worked out alright. Talk to you soon." She hung up.

"Tell me that wasn't Melody. Did she hate me?"

"She thought you were cute and funny. You should try calling her, sounds like she wants to see you again."

A warm feeling creeped over me. Maybe things were working out as they were supposed to after all.

CHAPTER SEVENTEEN

T HAT NIGHT WHEN I got home, I didn't wait very long before reaching for the phone. Melody was just getting home from work but insisted she could talk. The minutes turned to hours, and our chemistry really began to reveal itself. She was a very interesting woman.

I think one of the things I appreciated most was her general interest in me. The most difficult part of the conversation was avoiding bringing up the Rorschach. It had been a pretty significant part of my life and I knew it was more than relevant, but how do you tell someone a story like that?

I did tell her all about Budd Dwyer. She remembered the whole thing from the news and asked me questions about my time as a journalist. It was getting close to time for me to get ready for bed when she brought something up that made me think.

"Did you read the paper today?"

"Nah. Since I stopped writing, I kind of stopped reading. Besides, it's never usually good news. People only want to read about the ugly side of society."

"Yeah, well, it's crazy how bad the city is getting. Some guy ran over a pregnant lady and then crashed into a tree. He was dead by the time the ambulance got there. But get this, they found a briefcase in his car with a huge bomb in it."

The feeling I had begun to associate with the ink consumed me. The feeling of something bigger, something speaking to me. "Briefcase? Did it say what his name was?"

"Uhm, I want to say Rod, or Rob, or something. Why?"

I found myself almost paralyzed.

"Lucas? What's up?"

"That guy was in my office today. He had the case with him. That bomb was inches away from me, sitting on my desk."

"No shit?"

"No, for real. What happened to the lady he hit?"

"Didn't really say. Airlifted to the hospital, I think. So sad."

I felt a lot of emotions all at once. I had to get off the phone. Considering I had a lethal device in my office hours earlier, Melody understood. "Keep in touch, Lucas."

I paced around the apartment, trying to sort my thoughts. That guy could have killed me, but he ran over a pregnant woman. How did she fit into the universe's plan? What did she do to get roped into this chaotic inkblot bullshit? What was that guy doing with the bomb? How many people would have died if I hadn't sent him to Claire? There were many questions I knew were completely rhetorical. There were no answers.

The rest of the night consisted of a lot of the same thing. My head spinning. I was getting so sick of asking myself what I was doing, yet I couldn't seem to shake Claire. The cure I was searching for in Melody was working, but it created almost as many issues as it resolved. How could I start a serious relationship with a base of dishonesty, even if it was dishonesty by means of omission of truth?

When I woke in the morning, I didn't feel very rested. I made my way into the office, and once again, Sophia was grinning at me. "Sounds like I'm a pretty good matchmaker."

I nodded. "She's super cool." I needed to talk, or at least say something. "Soph, can I ask you something?"

"Sure."

"If you had something going on in your life that was pretty significant, but also complicated, would you share it with someone you were trying to get to know?"

"Oh no, are you gay?"

I shook my head. How the hell did she come up with that conclusion? "No, never mind. It's nothing, really. You have today's files?"

She opened her drawer and pulled out the day's client files. "Whatever it is, honesty is always the best policy."

"Thanks." I took the folders and headed into my office. I sat at my desk and reviewed them, once again wondering if I would see anything as my day progressed. I hated that I found myself back to being haunted by the ink.

The rest of the day yielded no signs, and the night was similar to the one before. I spoke with Melody on the phone for a couple hours. She asked me about my experience with Rob, the bomb guy. It helped to talk about it, but it also made me feel like I wanted to open up about everything. I thought back to Claire and the obsession she developed when I shared the information about the Rorschach. I couldn't go through that again and decided that, for the time being, it would not be the topic of conversation.

The next day during my second appointment, I saw picture number two. A woman named Kristy was in to see me, and within the first twenty minutes I could tell she was suffering from postpartum depression. She had given birth to a young daughter a few weeks before and was having thoughts of harming her and her older brother.

I didn't realize I was talking to my second referral until she began to feel overheated and took off her sweater. The shirt she wore underneath was adorned with the picture of the cat that jumped out at me from the ink. As I listened to her story, I wondered what seeing Claire would do for her. I felt the same urge I had felt with Travis. I wanted to give my genuine assistance and not involve her in the chaos of the Rorschach.

By the end of the meeting, I had struggled with an internal debate and she could tell I was distracted. I thought about the man with the bomb and the kids that were victims of Travis's rage. I needed to trust the tests. What about the pregnant woman that Rob ran over?

"Are you even listening to me?"

I hadn't been. "Of course."

"So what do you think?"

With no idea what she said, and no idea how to answer, I acted on instinct. "What do you think about trying something a little different?" My words felt like fire as they escaped my lips. The look of hope in her eyes as I gave her Judith's number made me nauseous. I knew something horrible would be in her future, and I felt like I was responsible for it before it even happened.

When our session ended, I decided to call Judith. I figured maybe if I talked to her and let her know how I was feeling, maybe they would skip the cat lady.

"Hello?"

"Hey, Judith, it's Lucas."

"Please don't call here."

She hung up without even hearing what I had to say. Maybe it was the fact that Claire avoided me six days a week, or the fact I had Melody in my life, but I was getting pretty resentful. I felt like they held all the cards, no pun intended. I felt like I was being manipulated, and even if they did stab me in the back, I would have no idea how to even find them except a phone number.

I looked at the clock. My last appointment had a twenty minute lead on me, but I felt like I could still catch up. I jumped from my seat and left the office. "Hey, Soph, please cancel my last appointment for today. Something's come up."

"Are you alright? Where are you going?"

As I closed the door behind me, I yelled back over my shoulder. "All good, explain later."

I sped to my car, trying my best not to attract any attention to myself. I left the parking lot and headed down the street. I wasn't completely sure where I was going, but I hoped the woman would be trying to reach out to Claire right away. My instincts were right; about three blocks away, I saw her using a payphone. She had to be calling Judith.

I pulled over on the side of the road and slouched down in the driver's seat. The last thing I needed was for this woman to feel like her counselor was stalking her. When she hung up the receiver, she walked back toward her car. I just hoped she was heading straight to Claire's office, or morgue, or wherever she gave the tests from.

When the woman started driving, I followed her. I wasn't very good at that sort of thing, but I had seen enough bad television to know you should stay at least a couple of car lengths behind. She drove through the city a bit faster than she probably should have, but I was able to keep up.

It took about ten minutes before she signaled into a parking lot. I wasn't sure what to expect, but part of me was actually a little impressed. The outside of the building looked quite professional and well taken care of. It made me wonder how Claire was funded. Maybe she charged people for the tests, or maybe Judith was a cash cow. Either way, I was pretty sure I knew where they were operating from.

Just to be sure, I watched my client go to the door. It seemed Claire had only a small office in the large building. Before leaving, I decided to drive by and see if there was any kind of sign to advertise the business inside. I tried to go slow enough that I could read it but not so slow I was noticed by anyone. There was a small sign that read Psych Ink. Of course that's what she called it.

I left the lot and parked a block away on the street. I kept eyes on the woman's car and waited. I felt a bit like a cop on a stakeout, even though I figured I was doing something immoral, maybe even illegal. She was inside for about forty minutes, and when she came out she looked a bit more at ease than she had on her way in. I hoped that was a good sign.

I followed her again as she got back on the road. We drove another fifteen minutes until she pulled into an apartment complex. Once again I waited, feeling our adventures together had not yet come to a conclusion. Within ten minutes, she emerged from the building. She had a car seat in one arm and the hand of a small boy in the other.

She loaded the baby into the car and made sure both kids were strapped in. Nothing seemed out of the ordinary to me, and I wondered if maybe Claire had somehow shared my feelings and not administered the test. When she drove off again, I followed her. It seemed like she wasn't going anywhere in particular.

At one point, she made four left turns in a row. We ended up doing a big circle around a few blocks. I felt like she may have suspected I was tailing her and I debated giving up my campaign and heading back home to clear my head. But something told me to keep following her, so I did.

She pulled up to an intersection with a set of train tracks. There was a random car sandwiched between us. The arms were slowly moving down to stop traffic, and the red lights and loud noises began. I hated waiting for trains, but it was interesting to see all the spray paint on the sides of the cars when they were going slow enough.

I could tell this particular train was not moving slowly at all. It became obvious what she was doing when my client drove through the wooden arms and stopped her car on the tracks. Knowing she had two children on board, I jumped out of my vehicle and ran toward her. It was too late.

The sound of the train smashing into the car was something I could never forget. It launched it into the air, and pieces of debris rained down like hail for the briefest of moments. When the wreckage rolled past me, something flew out of the mutilated back door and landed near my feet. I looked down with horror as I saw it was the arm, shoulder, and part of the head of the newborn baby.

I froze as I stared at it. It was enough I could identify what it was but not enough it could even been classified as a body. A small amount of blood pooled around it, but in a situation like that, there wasn't much left. I barely even noticed the crowd of people screaming and freaking out around me. The police and ambulance sirens were muted in my head. All I could focus on was this lifeless, little, partial baby and the fact I saw it coming and that it may have even been my fault for interfering with the test.

Chapter Eighteen

I CALLED MELODY AS soon as I knew she was home from work. I told her about what happened, omitting that I had been following the victim and that she had been my client. It was hard to really understand what was going on without being able to tell her everything, but I wasn't ready. I was really starting to care for her, and I didn't want to involve her in the nightmare of the Rorschach.

She tried to be as supportive as possible and even shared some personal stories with me to try to relate. From my limited observation of her, she was typically pretty lighthearted, and it was the most serious I had ever really heard her. It made me want more connection. I told her I felt guilty, like I should have done more. She reassured me that someone else's decisions weren't my fault. In my mind, I wasn't so sure.

Maybe one of the inkblots depicted me. Maybe she saw me following her and it triggered something the world wasn't ready to understand. Something that Melody wasn't ready to understand. Something that I really didn't even understand. Now I was back to feeling crazy.

I didn't sleep much at all that night and called Sophia the next morning. I explained what I had seen and told her I wouldn't be in. I guess the impact of my story caused her to forget about my sudden departure the day before because she never even mentioned it.

About a minute after I hung up with Sophia, my phone rang. "Hello?"

"How are you feeling? Get any sleep?" It was Melody.

I ran my fingers through my hair and sighed. "No, not really. Called in sick to work today. I think that's the first time I've ever done that."

"That doesn't surprise me. Want to play hooky together?"

"You would do that?"

"Not everyone has an aversion to calling in sick, Lucas. Of course I'll do that. You had a really fucked up day yesterday."

"I appreciate that. What are you thinking?"

"I'm thinking I will come over with a bottle of rum and we'll do some day drinking to forget our problems."

I was caught a bit off guard. "Oh, uhm, yeah, okay."

"See you in about an hour. I have to call my boss and get ready."

She hung up, and my focus changed instantly. She really cared about me, and now she was getting ready to come over. I felt so elated that everything disappeared for about fifteen seconds. Then I remembered how Claire made me feel. I remembered my wild mood swings and questioned myself again. Most people didn't sway that quickly from devastated to excited.

The whole thing was wearing on me. I knew I was different, but I wasn't a psychopath. I had feelings and emotions, and when that test wasn't in my life, I had the ability to function as a normal, contributing member of society. No, I had a master's degree and my own practice. I was able to *excel* as a normal member of society.

What was really going on? Had I been chosen by the universe to implement its will? Had I become some sort of vigilante enforcer of fate? Was I special, or was I just another guy who was going to end up in an institution rambling about something that made no sense to anyone else? I wished I had answers, and the only thing that had ever given me any real clarity before was the Rorschach. The very idea seemed not only counter-productive, but insane.

I shook my head and brought myself back to reality. I shaved and had a shower. I made my bed and tidied up my apartment in anticipation of Melody's arrival. I had no idea how I should be feeling or presenting when she got there. Was she going to want to sleep with me? Would that make me a slime ball? I hated how much I tended to overthink.

I sat on the couch and turned on the television. The news was on, and it was covering the story from the day before. My reality kicked me in the face again, and I started to cry as I thought about the two young children that perished in the ordeal. I stood up to change the channel, but at the same time, I heard a knocking at my door.

I wiped my eyes and put on my best "I'm okay" façade. When I opened the door, I could tell she wasn't fooled. She gave me a big hug before she even took her shoes off. "I'm so sorry, Lucas."

I held her tight; it felt comforting. I wept uncontrollably. I felt almost lucky that I had the excuse of the trauma from the previous day. I was so full, and that experience was only a small portion of the weight that filled me. In the moment that she embraced me, it all poured out and I couldn't stop. When we finally separated, I felt lighter.

I wiped my eyes as quickly as I could and tried to regain my composure. "Sorry. Thanks for coming."

"Of course. Are you alright?"

I nodded. "Yeah. Sorry, I'm not sure what happened there."

She stood there for a second and stared at me. "Can I come in?"

Realizing she was still standing at the door and I was blocking her way, I laughed a little. "Of course." I stepped back to allow her into my space.

She looked around with a few nods of approval. "Nice place. Not sure about that ugly rug, though."

I looked down at the throw rug that still concealed the remnants of Keith's blood. "That is a whole other story that we probably don't want to get into right now." I laughed, but I could tell she saw the sincerity in my statement.

"You're a bit of an enigma, Lucas. I feel like we've gotten to know each other really well in the short time we've been talking, but sometimes I feel like there's a whole other side of you that you keep locked away."

Her perceptions were impressive, but I knew I couldn't tell her that. "I try to be transparent. Did you say something about day drinking?"

She reached into her purse and pulled out a bottle of rum. "Ta-da."

I smiled and wiped my eyes again. I wanted to try to get back into an optimistic mindset, and I hoped the combination of the woman and the bottle in front of me could do just that. I grabbed a couple small glasses from the kitchen, and we sat together on the couch.

She opened the bottle and poured a shot into each glass. "Want to talk about what's bothering you, or do you want to just watch a movie and get smashed?"

I took the glass off the table and pounded it back. It was a lot stronger than I anticipated. I grimaced and almost threw up. So much for my plan of looking cool. "Let's start with drinking." I stood up and pulled a VHS tape from my TV cabinet. "Seen this one yet?"

She poured another glass for each of us after taking her own without flinching. "The Crow? What's it about?"

"It's about a vigilante. The guy really died when they were making it."

"I like a good vigilante story, throw it on."

I slid the tape into the VCR and sat back on the couch. We kept the conversation to a minimum as we watched. She poured drinks but ended up giving herself two for every one she gave me. I guess she didn't want me to get too drunk too fast and pass out or throw up again.

As the movie progressed, she continued to inch closer to me. Her hand ended up on my lap, and before I knew it, we were kissing. It felt right. Things kept going in that direction until I invited her to my bedroom. As we made our way there, hand in hand, I snapped back into a reality I didn't want to think about. I hadn't been with anyone other than Claire since high school, and now I was going to sleep with another woman in the bed we had shared together.

When Melody took her shirt off, I forgot all about it. We explored each other's bodies and let everything happen. It could have been the alcohol, but I'm pretty sure I was able to last quite a while and perform well. In hindsight it's hard to say, but regardless, we both had a good time. Once we were satisfied, we stayed in bed and fell asleep in each other's arms.

I woke up in a bit of a panic, thinking I was late for work. I realized it was eleven-thirty in the morning and felt at ease as I remembered what was going on. I woke her up when I sat up to look at my alarm clock. She looked as confused as me. I kissed her on the forehead. "Hey."

"Hey. What time is it?"

"Eleven-thirty."

She sat up and stretched. "I think I need a coffee before I start drinking again. You?"

"I could use one. I still feel drunk, though."

She slid out of bed and got dressed. Her body was beautiful. I always found a woman more attractive when she revealed a stunning personality. The thought occurred to me that I had no desire for Claire the last time she had stopped by. When someone does ugly things, they look ugly. When someone shows up when you need them, like Melody, their beauty only intensifies.

I followed her lead and rolled out of bed. When I got dressed, I noticed I had put on my work pants. Force of habit. We headed outside and got in her car. Shewas a bit wobbly. "Are you alright to drive?"

"Oh, yeah." She opened the door, and I followed suit. The drive to the coffee shop seemed to back up her statement that she was fine behind the wheel. When we went inside, I stumbled a couple of times. Whenwe got to the counter, I reached into my pocket to find some money to pay. I pulled out the slip of paper with Judith's number on it. My work pants. Damn it.

After Melody paid for the drinks, we got back in the car. "That movie was good. Do you think that some people deserve to die? Like, if they're bad?"

I shrugged. It seemed like a very strange coincidence she was asking this right after I realized I had Judith's number in my pocket. But I was sure that's all it was, coincidence. "Depends what they did, I guess. Do you?"

She started backing up out of the parking space. "Fuck, yeah. We need more people that are willing to stand up for the little guy."

We had only moved about three feet when I heard a loud bang. I turned around to see Melody had backed into someone who was walking away from the establishment.

"Watch it, you fucking moron!" He tossed his drink at the car, and it exploded on the back windshield. That's when I saw it. It was the third image. The random splotch I couldn't identify revealed itself to me when I was least expecting it. With all the talk of vigilantism and the knowledge I had, I made an impulsive decision.

I got out of the car and headed toward him. "Hey man, she barely touched you. We're sorry, alright?"

"I should fucking sue you!"

"I'll make it up to you, okay?" I reached in my pocket and pulled out Judith's number. "Call this lady, she will sort this all out."

Though it was clear he wasn't satisfied, he actually took the paper and walked away. Maybe the alcohol was intensifying my confidence in the Rorschach, but I knew in my heart he would accept it. I knew he would call. Despite all my attempts to discredit the test, it had an element of power I could never understand. I felt that energy, and I knew the man Melody hit was feeling it too.

I knew he was going against his better judgment by accepting the card. I knew he would rather fight me than walk away. But I also knew the situation would end like it did if I just trusted the process and followed the flow of the universe. It worked. I got back in the car.

"Holy shit, what did you say to that guy to get him to go away?"

I shrugged. "Sometimes you just have to be stern with those kinds of people."

"You're my hero." She smiled with exaggeration before checking her mirrors. She backed up, then pulled back onto the road, back toward my apartment.

CHAPTER NINETEEN

WHEN WE GOT BACK to my place, the first thing she went for was the bottle. She hadn't even opened her coffee before she was pouring more rum. I sat beside her on the couch and put my hand on her knee. "You alright?"

She had a bit of a glazed look on her face. "Can I ask you something?"

"Sure."

"The other night..." She took a deep breath. "When I dropped you off, there was a woman here. It looked very much like she was waiting for you."

My heart sank. That was the last question I wanted her to ask. I sucked at lying. "Yeah, she was."

She tensed up a little. "I didn't feel like it was my place to ask, but now things are a little different."

"Right." I paused and tried to think. I decided to be as honest as I could. "Her name is Claire. We have a business arrangement, and she was here to talk to me about it."

"At eleven thirty at night? Look, Lucas, I'm not the jealous type, but I'm starting to get some feelings. I don't want to be hurt. Please tell me, are you sleeping with her?"

My heart was racing. Technically I wasn't sleeping with her, at least not anymore. I hadn't even touched her since I met Melody. "No."

"That's pretty vague." She pounded her entire glass of rum and filled it back up. She poured another for me too. "Please, just tell me what the deal is so I'm not stuck speculating."

I took the glass and drank all the contents. It still burned and made me flinch, but it was getting easier. "Alright. She was my girlfriend at one time. We lived together, and one day I woke up and she was gone. She showed up a little while ago and roped me into a business agreement."

"What kind of business agreement?"

I sighed. "Melody, I really don't want to lie to you. Please just trust me that I'm not sleeping with her and you have nothing to worry about."

"Why would you need to lie to me? What's the big secret with this chick?"

I put my glass out and motioned for more rum. "She's dangerous."

She filled my glass about an inch, then filled hers about three. "Dangerous? Lucas, I can take care of myself. I'm not worried about some scrawny little bitch who used to bang you. What makes her so scary?"

I took my drink; there was even less burn than the one before. "Remember when you first came over? You pointed out the rug?"

"Yeah, so?"

"Go lift it up."

She shot back her drink and set the glass on the table. She looked at me with a bit of suspicion. "Alright, I will." She got up and went over to the throw rug, reaching down and pulling hard on two of the corners. She held it in the air with both hands as she looked at the dark stains underneath. "What is that?"

"Blood."

"Who's blood?"

"Some of it's mine. Some of it belongs to an ex-boyfriend of Claire's named Keith."

She dropped the rug back on the floor and made her way over to the couch. She poured another two fingers of rum before sitting back down beside me. "Jesus. What the hell happened?"

"He came here looking for her in the middle of the night. When I went to investigate, he attacked me, and then Claire shot him in my living room."

"Did she get arrested?"

"We both got questioned. It was self defense. The guy had no right to be here, and he broke in." I put my hand on her knee again. "But Claire, she had this aura about her. It was so easy for her to pull that trigger, and even after it happened, it didn't seem to even phase her. I watched a woman and her kids get killed by a train and I can't even go to work. She didn't seem to care about her situation one way or the other."

"I think I need another nap." She emptied her glass and spread out across the couch.

I squeezed in beside her. I was definitely drunk and tired, but my mind was racing. I felt like I had told her at least eighty percent of the truth. I wished I could tell her more, but involving someone else in my nightmare didn't seem fair. Keeping secrets didn't seem fair. Once again, it felt like Claire was running my life. If it wasn't for her and that fucking Rorschach, I could be in a normal relationship and living a normal life.

I could feel her breathing getting deeper. I ran my fingers through her long red hair. It was so soft. I moved it out of her face and admired her beauty for a few minutes. I knew I wanted the relationship to work, and to do that, I needed some guidance. I also knew where to find it, but the thought seemed so counterproductive. If I needed direction, I needed Claire. I needed the Rorschach.

With Melody's soothing breaths and the alcohol in my system, I fell asleep on the couch. When I woke up, she was gone. I checked the time, and it was almost nine at night. The rug had been moved again. I wasn't sure if that was the way it had landed or if she looked at the stains again before she left. I readjusted it to its original spot. I could tell I was still a bit drunk, the downfall of being a lightweight.

I figured I should go to work the next day, so I did my best to get motivated. I had a cold shower and tried to sort my thoughts. I had seen all three of the last images, but I didn't know for sure if the last guy had even called Judith. Either way, I did my part, so I expected to see Claire in the near future.

I emerged from the shower and wrapped myself in a towel. I stared into the mirror for a few minutes and tried to think sober thoughts. I had a plan, but was it a good plan? My intuition was guiding me, but I still couldn't positively identify the driving force behind it. I knew there were some answers I would never get, especially when it came to fate. The universe. God. Whatever.

I snapped out of my thoughts when I heard a noise coming from the living room. I opened the bathroom door with the anticipation of seeing Melody. Claire stood there staring at the throw rug. "You moved it."

"How can you tell? What are you doing here?"

She kept her eyes on the floor. "You know why I'm here. Why did you move the rug?"

"It was a vacuum day. How did you get in here?"

"You left your door unlocked. You had her over, didn't you? That woman from the other night?"

The shower helped, but I was still feeling a bit intoxicated, tired, and confused. "I don't want to play games, Claire."

"Did you fuck her?"

"Excuse me?"

"Ahh, you did. Good for you." She took a few steps toward me and eyed me up and down.

I felt a bit self conscious standing there in nothing but a towel. "Why do you care?"

"I thought we really had something. I thought you felt it too."

"Yeah, well, I can only get ghosted and heartbroken so many times before I lose interest. Did you bring the test?"

She held her handbag slightly in the air. "Yep, it's right in here. Did you tell her about it? Did you tell her about me?"

"I told her about you. That's it."

"Really? Good things, I hope?"

"What else could I say, Claire?"

She smirked. "Right. Maybe you aren't looking for any advice from me, but if I were you, I wouldn't get too deep into the details of our arrangement. The Rorschach is a complicated thing, as you know. I feel like it may not take too kindly to strangers being made aware of its existence."

"Is that a threat?"

"Take it as you will. I'm only giving you advice. It's not like I can see the future."

It was strange to see her in such a different light. Instead of being alluring and beautiful, she looked manipulative and repulsive. I don't know how to explain it, but everything changed in that instant. Her hazel eyes became chestnut pits that led to the depths of Hell instead of gateways to a magical soul. Her beauty faded to that of an insect looking for its next meal of blood. I had to keep my cards close to my chest. "Give me a minute to get dressed."

"We won't be long. You're not going to try and back out of this test, are you?"

I stared at her for a second. It was strange to see a rival instead of any ally. I wasn't sure if it was the alcohol, me, or the universe, so I decided to be conservative with my words. "I won't back out, but I do have a condition."

"You have a condition? That's cute. What is it?"

"I want to administer the test myself. Alone."

She got a puzzled look on her face. "Why?"

"What difference does it make? You want referrals, I want to do the test alone. Leave and come back in twenty minutes."

"Are you planning on stealing it?"

"Seriously? There is one door to this place. I presume you will be standing by it."

"So you plan on destroying it?"

"We both know that doesn't work."

"What then?"

"I don't want to see you when I do it."

"You know you're the only one that can see the pictures anyway."

"I know everything about these tests, Claire. I'm the one who the gypsy gave them to. Remember?"

She nodded. I could tell she was skeptical, but I also knew she could tell she had lost her leverage. My undying love for her had always been a surefire way of control, and I think she was struggling without it. "Alright, fine. I'll be back in twenty minutes. You better actually do it."

I took the three papers and the vial from her and headed toward the table. She made her way to the front door. I pulled out the small knife I always used and waited for her to leave. Once the door was closed firmly, I opened the inkwell and slid the small blade along the tip of my finger. I squeezed three drops into the vial.

I placed a single drop on each sheet, and as usual, the pictures emerged. The first was a pair of fuzzy dice. The second, a brick. Image number three looked like a squirrel.

Having completed the test, it was time to seek some answers for myself. Since Claire had come back in my life, I was only seeing images related to others. I needed guidance; I needed clarity. I needed a second test. A test for me, not for Claire or the universe. I had never done two in the same day before, or even done one before the previous images had revealed themselves. I didn't even know if it would work, but I had to try.

I placed the knife back on my finger and re-opened the wound. I dripped three more drops into the ink. I took a deep breath and looked at the cards. They were all blank again. One more drop for each piece.

The first looked to be a hypodermic needle.

The second caught me off guard. It was a pair of breasts. They were breasts I recognized. They were Claire's.

The third initially looked like a soda can that had been partially squished. As I looked closer, I could tell it was a spent round. A bullet that had likely been used to kill someone.

I wasn't sure what I was dealing with, but I knew I had committed myself to six new images. I wasn't even sure if Claire had ever tried doing that. I piled the papers back up and sealed the inkwell. I stood from the table and took a few steps toward my room to get some clothes on. I didn't make it very far before the door opened.

"All done, Mr. Secretpants?"

I pointed to the table. "All done, and there they are. Not destroyed or stolen or anything."

She picked everything up and putting it back in her purse. "Did you spit on them?" She was trying to be cheeky and cute. It made my stomach turn a little.

"I'm going to get dressed now. We're done here?"

She stepped closer again. "You feeling underdressed? Would this help?" She pulled her shirt off in a swift motion. Her breasts exposed.

I was already seeing an image from the tests. I was a bit confused as to why it wasn't the first image. I had to remind myself that I really didn't know how the ink worked. I stared at her chest, but not with lust. I knew she was trying to use sex to gain control again. She was intimidated by my relationship with Melody, and she wanted to fuck it up. "I'm sorry, Claire. I can't."

She got a look on her face I had never seen before. I could tell she was frustrated and insulted. "What the fuck, Lucas?"

"I'm in a relationship now. I'm sorry. Please leave."

She shook her head in frustration and put her shirt back on. She left without saying another word and slammed the door behind her.

Chapter Twenty

I WOKE IN THE morning to the sound of my alarm. I felt tired and groggy, but I forced myself out of bed. When you own your own business, you don't want to take too many days off. I also knew I needed to keep the referrals going for Claire if I wanted to keep her off my back. I knew I already pissed her off the night before.

I stumbled through my morning routine and made my way to work. I felt like I was on very high alert, especially since I had already seen one of the images. I arrived at work to find Sophia at her desk, looking somber.

"Hey, Lucas, are you alright?"

It actually took me a second to remember the train crash. It made me realize how messed up my life was getting. How can someone even come close to forgetting something so tragic? "Hey, Soph, much better. Thanks. How are you?"

"I missed you yesterday, but I'm alright. Here's your files for today."

I took the files from her and nodded. "Thanks."

"Hey, if you need to talk, I'm here. Okay?"

I forced a smile. "Thanks. I know you are."

I headed into my office and sat at my chair. I had only been off for a day, but it seemed like a lot had happened in that short time. I tried to focus on work, but as the day went on, I found myself again searching for images I knew had to appear organically. I was off my game, and I was pretty sure my clients could tell.

Though I had a lot on my mind, my thoughts continued to drift back to Melody. I wondered why she had left. I debated being completely open with her. Claire was telling me not to, but I was sure that had more to do with her own personal jealousy and insecurity than it actually did with me potentially pissing off a bottle of ink and a few papers.

On my lunch break, Sophia tried to come in and console me about the whole train wreck thing. I was so focused on the phone that I either caused her more concern or made her feel dismissed. Either way, she didn't stick around too long, and as soon as the door closed, I picked up the receiver and called Melody.

"Hello?"

"Hey. I woke up and you were gone. Everything alright?"

"Yeah. Just a bit emotional about your ex. Trying to wrap my head around it. I'm really worried about being hurt, Lucas."

"I know. I am too. How about we meet tonight after work? Same place as we had our first date?"

She paused for a minute. "Alright, I would like that."

"See you at seven." I hung up feeling much better. I felt like the fact Claire didn't want me to do something was almost enough reason on its own to do it. I was going to tell Melody everything and let the chips fall where they may. I didn't feel I had a lot to lose.

The rest of the work day produced no new images. I was alright with that, but part of me worried that no referrals would cause Claire to think I was up to something. I had to remind myself Claire shouldn't be my focus, Melody should. When I left the office, I had a bit of an ominous feeling. I couldn't quite place it, but it almost felt like I was being watched.

I looked around and didn't see anything suspicious, so I tried to pass it off as my imagination. I drove home and got ready to meet with Melody. When I left my apartment, the feeling returned. I did a pretty thorough visual around the parking lot, but nothing stood out. As I made my way to the bar, a thought occurred to me. The woman I was following made four left turns. Nobody would do that. If you thought you were being followed, though, it would be a sure way to verify it.

I put on my blinker and turned left. I kept my eyes on the rearview as much as I could without crashing into something. A black sedan with dark tinted windows made the same turn. At the next block, I repeated the same action. Once again, it turned, now following a couple car lengths behind. When I hit the next block and put my signal on for a third time, it continued going straight. All in my head.

I pulled up to the pub and parked my car. Before I went inside, I double checked nobody was following me. I was having a hard time shaking the feeling, but I figured it was just because I felt like I was doing something wrong by defying Claire. Like I was a small kid shoplifting for the first time and checking everywhere for cameras.

When I got inside, Melody was already sitting down. She had a glass of rum in front of her and looked like she hadn't slept. "Hey, you. You look good."

"Let's not start this off with lies, Lucas. I know I look like shit."

"I'm not lying." I really wasn't. It was strange that even when she looked rough, she still looked gorgeous to me. It was like her inner beauty shined a light on her exterior that overshadowed the dark bags under her eyes.

"I don't know what you're going to tell me. To be honest, I'm worried. Is this going to be all about some sex cult or something? Orgy's with animal blood or human sacrifice?"

"When you put it that way, maybe it's not so bad after all."

I took a deep breath and started from the beginning. I started by retelling the story of January 22, 1987. Budd Dwyer. I told her about the gypsy, the strange energy that compelled me and, of course, the Rorschach.

I went into detail about my job at the suicide hotline, and even about Chad. I tried to downplay it, but the truth was that I pushed the man off a cliff. I was a bit surprised she seemed more interested than appalled. I told her everything all the way up to the present day. She didn't speak a word and didn't order any more drinks. It took over an hour to share all the elements.

When I was done, I looked at her for some kind of reaction. We sat in silence for a minute, then she got up and walked toward the door. "Melody, wait."

She didn't look back. By the time she got to the door, I was up and following her. I followed her outside and watched her get in her car. I was waiting for her to drive away, but she didn't. She didn't even turn the key; she just sat there. Though I could read a client like a book, for some reason when it came to women I struggled to pick up their signals. I felt like she wanted me to join her.

I approached her car, and when she still didn't start it, I reached for the passenger door. I opened it slowly and looked inside. She was just staring ahead. "Can I sit with you?"

She nodded but remained silent. I sat down and noticed something I hadn't before. There was a pair of fuzzy dice hanging from her rearview mirror. Not just any dice, but the pair I saw in the ink. "Were those always there?"

She looked at me with a bit of confusion. "Seriously?"

"I need to know."

"They've always been in my car, but they fell down. I found them in the back seat this morning and put them back up. Is that enough information about my car accessories now that we've finished talking about some supernatural murder test?"

I could feel tears forming in my eyes. "I saw those dice in the ink. Last night."

"What does that mean?"

"I don't know. It was in the first test that I did. If it wants me to refer you to Claire, it can fuck right off."

Her eyes widened. "Wait a minute..."

"What?"

She looked at me with a bit of a sinister smile. It was the first emotion I had really seen from her since I started my story. I knew what she was thinking. "No, Melody."

"Yes, Lucas."

"You don't know what all this shit does to you. You need to trust me."

"If you want me to trust you, Lucas, to really trust you, give me the number."

"Why would you possibly want that?"

"I need to see it for myself. You mentioned how many times that you thought you were crazy. I have to be honest, I'm thinking you weren't far off. If you actually want me to believe all of this, then I need to take the test myself."

I put my hands over my face and pressed the back of my head against the seat. I didn't want any interaction between Claire and Melody, and it never even dawned on me she would be a potential referral. "People die when someone does that test, Melody."

"You're already forgetting your own bullshit, Lucas. You said the first time you took it nothing bad happened. That seems a little inconsistent. Claire too. It wasn't until the second test that people died. I'm only asking to do one. I need to experience this compulsion and lack of freewill. If you want our relationship to work, then you need to do this or I'll always wonder what you're really hiding."

I took a second to think. It was insane, but at the same time, it made sense. It reminded me of everything else in my life.

"Do you know someone who drives a black car?"

"What?"

"That car." She motioned with her eyes across the parking lot. "It's been sitting there the whole time we've been out here."

As though the driver of the other vehicle could hear us, the engine started and it pulled out. The car looked like the same one that had followed me for two left turns on my way over. I caught a glimpse of the driver and knew right away it was Judith. "Fucking Claire."

"That was her?"

"No, her assistant. Judith. If I give you the number, she'll be the one to answer the phone."

A look of frustration came over her. "Fuck, that means she knows what I look like. I do admit that the fact that she's obviously stalking us does add some credit to your story. Of course, she could just be another one of your satanic sex friends trying to protect her secrets."

"You're kidding, right?"

"Mostly. Fuck, I need to come up with a new plan. I still need her number, though."

I was reluctant, but I wrote down Judith's number. I had done so enough times I had it memorized. "You need to be careful with this. I'm not kidding."

"That lady probably followed you here from your apartment, maybe even your work, and you didn't catch on. You don't need to tell me to be careful, Columbo."

"I had a feeling I was being followed."

"Yeah, a lot of good that did." She rubbed her eyes. "Look, I'm sorry Lucas. I want to believe you, I really do. I'm not trying to be mean, but this whole thing is kind of a lot to absorb."

"I get it."

"Alright. I'll figure out how I'm going to handle this. Let me know if anything comes up that I need to know."

I nodded. I wanted to lean over and kiss her, but I didn't want to push my luck. The fact she heard me out and was willing to at least try to accept it as the truth was a good enough starting point. "Talk soon. Thanks for listening." I opened the door and got out, making my way back to my own car to drive home alone.

CHAPTER
TWENTY-ONE

W HEN MY ALARM WENT off, I wanted nothing more
than to turn it off and go back to sleep. It had
been a long night. But I didn't want to miss work. As
I was getting dressed and ready, I thought about what
Melody had said. I obviously had been followed for a
significant amount of time and had no idea. Either Judith
was a professional stalker or I sucked at observing my
surroundings. Either way, I decided I needed to be more
vigilant.

That morning, I must have looked around every
corner and over my shoulder more times than a meth
addict. I'm sure if anyone had seen me, they likely would
have labeled me as a man with serious mental health
issues. It didn't make me feel much safer; if anything, I
felt more paranoid.

When I made it to work, I felt a bit more at ease. The
office felt like a safe zone for me. Sophia was at her desk.
"Good morning. Are You alright?"

"I had a rough night. Is it that obvious?"

"Things not going well with Melody? Last we spoke she seemed pretty into you."

"Yeah, things are alright. Just feeling a bit paranoid."

She smiled. "Just because you're paranoid don't mean they're not after you."

"What?"

"It's a song. Never mind. You want to talk about it?"

I sighed. The last thing I needed was to involve Sophia in any of my drama. "I'm alright. You have the files for today?"

I could tell she felt a little disappointed. We always shared details about our personal lives, and I knew it probably seemed I was shutting her out. I couldn't exactly tell her it was for her own safety and then not elaborate. Silence could be golden.

"Alright. I hope at some point we can talk about whatever is going on with you. You have Terry this morning, and then your afternoon is Chris, and then Barbara."

My eyes widened and I knew she could tell. "Barbara?"

"Yeah, she was here not too long ago. She called to set a follow up. Something wrong?"

Something was very wrong. "No, just curious." I took the files. "Thanks, Soph."

"Your hands are shaking."

I tried to smile. "Yeah, a lot of coffee this morning to make up for a bad sleep."

I headed into the office and closed the door. I looked at the clock and saw I had about thirty minutes before my first appointment. I tried calling Judith to find out what was going on. She didn't answer. I tried again and got the same result. I knew I had to stay focused and not let my clients see me shaken. I leafed through Terry's file and tried to get myself prepared.

He arrived on time and sat across from me. I did my best to listen and use the skills I knew I had, but I couldn't get Claire off my mind. Why was she coming in for another appointment? I hadn't sent her all the referrals yet. Why would she come to my office and not my apartment if she was worried about people seeing us together?

"Are you even listening to me?"

I had gotten lost in my thoughts. "Of course, Terry. I'm so sorry."

"Right, so should I kill the cat?"

I had to pretend like I knew what he was talking about. "Of course not, why would you kill it?"

"Obviously so it doesn't try and rape me again. Are you sure you're paying attention?"

It was around that time I realized how much Claire had gotten into my head. Maybe that was her intention. Maybe she wouldn't even show up. I brought myself back to the present and finished a strange session with Terry. When he left, I had the impression he wouldn't be booking a follow up, but I was all right with that.

Over my lunch break, I tried calling Judith again, and again she didn't answer. I told myself Claire was just messing with me and carried on with my day as best I could. My next client, Chris, threatened to leave during our session if I didn't pay more attention. Again I had to try to refocus and stay out of my head. During our last half hour, he called me out on looking at the clock every five minutes.

"Do you have a hot date or something?"

"Sorry, I'm with you."

"Yeah, well, it's close enough. I'm out of here."

Part of me felt horrible about not giving a client my full attention, but another part of me was relieved. I didn't want a reputation as a clinician that didn't care to listen, but Claire was burrowed into my brain like a parasite. I needed to know what she wanted. She must have had some sort of plan or motive for booking in. I couldn't focus on anything else until I knew what her agenda was.

When I heard the front door open, my stomach went into knots. My office door was mostly closed, but I could hear her talking with Sophia. It was Claire.

"Good morning, dear."

"You're in luck, Barbara. His last client left a little early. You can go right in."

Over the years, I had felt a lot of things in regards to Claire, but that was the first time I felt nervous. Maybe even a little afraid. When I saw the door open, I could feel bile rising in my throat and my chest felt like it was about to explode. I was confused by my reaction, but I knew my instincts were usually pretty accurate.

When she came into the room, she looked different to me. Her hair was darker, and it made her eyes less vibrant. The beauty that once radiated off her now gave me chills. I felt like I was looking at a troll.

"Hello, Lucas. Thanks for seeing me again."

"Why are you here?"

"Aren't you going to make Barbara jokes and be all cute?"

"No."

She smiled. "Aren't you going to ask me about my hair?" She ran her hand through her locks and exaggerated them.

"I know you're here for a reason. It'sbeen bugging me all day. Just tell me what you want."

Her demeanor became more serious and professional. "Fine. I'm only here as a friend. I have some information for you that I felt like I should share."

"A friend, huh? Alright, what do you want to share with me?"

"Does the name Curtis Cormier sound familiar?"

I paused for a moment to think. "No."

"Really? You sent him to me a few days ago. Apparently your little girlfriend nearly killed him in the parking lot of a coffee shop."

Things became clear pretty quickly. "She didn't almost kill him. The guy walked right behind us as we were pulling out."

"Well, that's not how he sees it. Anyway, he took your advice and called us."

"And?"

"Well, he was pretty fixated on the whole car accident thing. He saw something in the cards that seemed to spark an idea or something."

My focus shifted to Melody. I felt like Claire was making some sort of threat. "It wasn't even an accident. What did he see?"

"You know as well as I do that the only person who can see the images is the one having the test done. I just got the impression that he may be planning on going after her. Maybe he saw something that could help him locate her? Maybe a plate number or something? You know how the test works. It's very cryptic sometimes."

I wanted to jump up and reach across my desk for her throat. I knew exactly what she was doing, but I needed to keep my wits about me. "Why does it sound like you're making threats? Is this related to me refusing your advances?"

She got a look of shock on her face. I couldn't tell if it was real or not. "Lucas, I'm here to do you a favor. I saw what I saw, and I'm worried that the little tramp may be in danger. That's it." She stood from her chair. "If you're going to make it seem like I know more than I do, I don't see any reason to continue this conversation."

"Why hasn't Judith been answering the phone?"

She took a couple steps toward the door and didn't even look at me as she spoke. "She's got the day off."

I reached for the phone to call Melody as soon as Claire was out of my office. I put the receiver back down when I heard her talking to Sophia.

"Have a good day, Barbara."

"See you soon, Sophia."

"What do you mean?"

"I'm friends with Judith. You called to set up a tarot reading."

"Oh right, I didn't know you guys knew each other. See you soon, I guess."

I jumped to my feet and hurried out of my office. The door clicked as it closed behind Claire. I looked over at Sophia with wide eyes. "Soph, you cannot meet with that woman. Promise me."

Sophia had a pencil in her hand and slammed it on the desk. She stared at me for a second before she spoke.

"Lucas, you have left me in the dark about everything, and now you're going to try and tell me what I can and can't do on my days off?"

I sighed loudly. "Soph, it's a lot, okay? You need to trust me that she is dangerous and you can't go see her. How did you even get her number?"

"Funny you should ask. Melody gave it to me and asked me to call. She didn't seem to want to elaborate on anything, either, but it was clear that it had something to do with you. Maybe if you fill me in I won't need to meet with this Judith lady to figure out what all the secrets are."

Melody. I ran back into my office and grabbed the phone. I dialed her number and listened to it ring. Sophia appeared at my door, watching me after I left our conversation so abruptly.

"Who are you calling?"

"Melody." The phone continued to ring with no answer.

"Lucas, what is going on?"

I hung up the phone and made my way back toward the door. "Soph, I have to go check on Melody." I paused in front of her. "I promise I will explain this, but please, just don't call Judith. Don't take any tests. Take the rest of the day off. I need to go."

She threw her arms in the air as I made my way by her. "What the hell, Lucas?"

I wished I had time to explain things to her, but after my meeting with Claire, I knew I needed to find Melody. I raced through the building and got into my car. The only place I thought I might find her would be her apartment. It was possible she was at work, but my instincts were telling me she wasn't.

I raced through traffic faster than I ever had before. I broke a few laws along the way and nearly caused an accident. I couldn't remember a time when anyone had honked their horn at me before, but that trip certainly made up for it in spades. When I started getting close, I tried to calm down, but I was frantic. Once again I felt completely insane. I was risking a speeding ticket or even a criminal charge with the way I was driving. Why? Because Claire made me feel like I should be worried.

When I arrived, I signaled to turn into her parking lot. Just as I began to pull in, a black sedan pulled onto the road. By that point, it was a car I recognized. There was no doubt in my mind Judith was behind the wheel. My instincts started screaming at me to hurry up and get to Melody's unit. My feeling went from panic to dread.

CHAPTER TWENTY-TWO

I WAS IN SUCH a hurry I nearly forgot to turn off my car before I got out. I walked with a fast stride toward the building and headed straight to Melody's apartment. I froze in my tracks for a moment when I saw the door was ajar. I took a deep breath before barging in.

Melody was lying on the couch with her arms crossed over her chest. I called to her as I made my way over, but she didn't move. I tried to shake her but there was still no response. I checked her pulse and couldn't find one. I could feel tears forming in my eyes as I tried to revive her. I couldn't lose her.

I needed help, and I needed it yesterday. I jumped up to find her phone but quickly noticed the cord had been cut. I turned to go back and start more attempts at resuscitation when I felt something around my neck. It was tight, like a wire or rope. I tried to struggle free but found myself lifted off the ground. It was digging into my throat, and after only a minute, I was struggling to breathe. My vision was getting hazy and my abilities to move were becoming limited.

As I lost the strength to stay on my feet, he lowered me down to my knees, and my hand brushed up against something on the table. With the last of my strength, I clenched it in my hand and swung it as hard as I could behind me. It was enough that I felt the rope around my neck give some slack and I was able to steal a breath. I swung it again and felt myself become free.

I turned to see Curtis standing there, holding his stomach. I looked in my hand to see a statue of Auguste Rodin's 'The Thinker'. I swung it again and hit him in the side of the head. He fell to the floor. I used the opportunity to try to catch my breath and get my bearings. I looked at the coffee table and saw a syringe that had clearly been used.

Melody didn't do drugs, at least not that I was aware of. Curtis must have overdosed her to make it look like something it wasn't. I glanced down at him; he was starting to come to. I needed answers I knew he wouldn't give me, so I did something impulsive. I grabbed him by both of his ankles and dragged him into the bathroom.

"What are you doing, man?"

I punched him in his face. I have to admit, it hurt my hand quite a bit, but it stunned him enough that I could hoist him into the bathtub. I did a quick survey of the room and picked up one of Melody's reusable leg razors. I opened it up and held the blade between my thumb and my index finger. I looked down at Curtis, who was dazed but awake. "I have a few questions for you."

"Fuck you."

I grabbed hold of his left ear and pulled it away from his head. I slid the razor along the inside; it went through like a hot knife through butter. I could feel the blood covering my hand, and it was like wearing a warm liquid mitten on a cold day. He screamed in pain, but I pushed his head up against the wall, dangling his ear in front of his face. "So? Questions?"

He spat in my face. I wiped if off and smiled before tossing his severed ear into the toilet next to the tub. I placed the edge of the razor on his cheek and applied pressure. I looked at him for a moment to give him a chance to start talking, but he just stared at me. I pressed the blade into his flesh, and it went through his cheek and into his mouth. With one quick slash, I dragged it out of the front of his mouth, leaving a flap of skin that revealed some of his teeth. He swatted at me with his hands but the loss of blood had already diminished his strength.

He screamed again, but I could tell he was trying not to. He was going for that cool "I can take any torture" kind of badass image. I can't say for sure what came over me, but I wanted to push him. I wanted to push him until he broke, and I was excited about it. I wanted to find some other weapons to use, but I knew I couldn't give him the chance to escape. I lifted his feet one at a time and took off his socks and shoes. I used the blade to make a tic-tac-toe patterns on the bottom of each foot that were at least an inch deep. I did my best to keep all the blood contained to the tub, but it was squirting out with a fair amount of force. I could feel it hitting my face, and I knew it was getting on the ceiling.

Just to make sure he wasn't going anywhere, I ran the blade deep into both of his Achilles tendons. He was biting down hard and growling in pain, but it seemed like he really didn't want to give me the satisfaction of crying or showing any weakness. I picked up Melody's hair straightener and used the cord to bound his hands behind his back.

I found it a bit funny that all he was really accomplishing was not alerting any neighbors to the festivities.

I made my way to the kitchen and found a large knife, a spoon, and a cheese grater. Feeling satisfied, I went back to the bathroom. I decided to start with the spoon. I pushed his head back against the wall and placed it against the bottom of his eye. "Soon, you could be a pirate. If you decide to talk to me and manage to live through this."

Right before I slid the utensil into his eye socket, he made a sudden move that caught me off guard. He pulled something from his pocket and tried to jab it into my neck. I was able to swat it away and heard it land on the tile floor. I stepped back and looked. It Was a hypodermic needle. The image flashed in my mind as the same one I saw in the ink.

With his efforts in vain, he started whimpering. I almost felt sorry for him, but then I thought of Melody lying lifeless in the next room.

"Alright, I'll talk."

I looked down at the floor, then back at him. "What's in the syringe?"

"Heroin. Enough to kill you."

"Claire sent you?"

He took some labored breaths. "No, Judith did. Claire doesn't even know I'm here."

I scoffed. "Well, that's bullshit." I leaned in and jammed the spoon into his eye socket. The tough-guy act was no longer an element. He screamed in pain as I dug around in his flesh. The eye was still hanging by some gross, stringy meat after I retracted the spoon.

"Please, stop!"

"Then tell me the truth. All of it."

He sobbed a bit more and started weeping from his good eye when he reached up to touch his face. "Alright. I went to that place, the one you sent me to, and I took the test. I saw a few pictures, and then I saw them in real life."

"I knew that much. How the fuck did you end up here?"

"Judith is crazy. The pictures from the ink made me think I needed to listen to her. She said she wanted this girl dead, and her boyfriend too. She told me to make it look like an accident."

"How does strangling someone look like an accident?"

"Man, I know cops. Two dead junkies are two dead junkies. Case closed." He winced in pain, and his voice was getting slower like he may pass out soon. "She didn't really tell my why, but it had something to do with her boss."

"What do you get out of this?"

"It's the universe, man. It was supposed to happen this way."

It was a bit refreshing to know I wasn't the only one the Rorschach affected so deeply. Looking down at the man that was slowly filling Melody's bathtub with blood almost gave me a bit of remorse. Almost. I still didn't completely trust him, and given the circumstances, I didn't think that to be overly unreasonable.

"You're leaving something out. We're just going to do this until you let me know what it is." I took the cheese grater and pressed it against his skin. I rubbed it down his arms, watching small bits of flesh tear away from his body and more blood gather in the ceramic basin.

He started screaming in pain and begging for respite. He got none until he decided to be honest. "Alright! It was Claire! I love her!"

I paused for a moment and pulled the grater away from his flesh. "You what?"

He spoke between sobs. "After the test, we hung out. I can't explain it, but there is something irresistible about her. She has an aura that I've never felt before. I love her, and she asked me to do this for her."

My suspicions were confirmed. Claire was jealous, or intimidated, or something. She played Curtis and got him to take care of the problem. She had used me and who knew how many others to gain more power. I felt stupid and angry. I picked up the kitchen knife and stabbed it with a single thrust into the man's heart. Blood poured out, and he fell limp.

I felt like I was well beyond the point of no return, but I had no idea what I was going to do. I needed something to send a message to Claire. I looked at the knife in my hand, then back at the lifeless man in the tub. A small souvenir would probably come in handy.

I'm not sure if you've ever tried to sever a human head with a kitchen knife, but it's not as easy as you may think. There are a lot of bones in the neck, and removing the head requires some finesse. Well, more like snapping and twisting and cutting. For future reference, in case you needed it, I got it off in about fifteen minutes.

I dropped the head in the tub and headed out to find something to put it in. I ended up with a pillow case and a garbage bag. I figured the pillow case would get nice and blood soaked and would add some dramatic effect for whatever I figured out I was going to do with it. The garbage bag would obviously prevent said blood from getting on my clothes or my car seats.

Before I left, I picked up the needle from the bathroom floor. It didn't have a cap, but I remembered seeing one on the coffee table with the other syringe. I was in a state of mind I wasn't used to. It reminded me of the whole incident with Chad. It was completely out of character for me, yet it didn't faze me at all. I was afraid of going back to the couch and seeing Melody. I didn't want to get back in touch with my emotions, and I knew her death was going to be difficult to process when I eventually returned to reality.

I took a deep breath and went for it. I tried not to look at her, but it was hard. I knew it would be the last time I ever saw her. She was beautiful, even in death. I really believed we could have had a future together, but I would never know. I picked up the bright orange cap and covered the sharp needle. I put it in my pocket and picked up the bag.

As I made my way back down to my car, I wasn't too worried about being seen. Maybe I felt like the end was near and nothing really mattered. Well, not nothing. What mattered was trying to come up with a plan to kill Claire. Judith was on my list as well, time permitting.

CHAPTER TWENTY-THREE

I DID EVERYTHING I could to get myself in a relatively rational state of mind. The only conclusion I could come to that made any sense was to go against my morals a little. I told myself I would never own a gun, but given the circumstances, I decided it was a necessity. I made my way back to a place I hadn't been to since I was with Claire—Sluggies.

I wasn't sure what to expect, walking back into that place. I pulled up nearby and parked the car, taking a deep breath before getting out. It felt a bit strange to be heading toward a gun shop and even stranger it wasn't my first time. I pushed the door open, and the bell rang as I entered.

Louie was working and didn't even look up as I approached the desk. He still had his mullet and mustache, and despite a few signs of aging, he basically looked exactly how I remembered him. He was engaged in a weapons magazine of some sort.

"Good afternoon, Louie."

He curled his lip and continued to read. "Whatcha need?"

"Well, I'm in a gun store. A gun perhaps?"

My sarcasm caught his attention. I could tell by the look on his face when we finally locked eyes his intentions were to either say something offensive or throw me out. Before he spoke, I saw the look of recognition replace the look of irritation. "I know you? You look familiar."

I pointed to the floor. "I killed a guy right there."

"Ah, damn. Didn't think I'd see you again. You looking for a new piece?"

I nodded. "Yeah, reluctantly. You have anything like the one I brought back?"

I could tell he got a bit lost in contemplation. He walked out from behind the counter and over to the front door. He switched the sign around to CLOSED, and a smile crept across his face. "How about the same gun?"

"You still have it?"

"Between you and me, I keep all the guns that have a body on 'em. If it's spilled blood, I save it. Normally it would stay with me forever, but since the body on that one is yours, I'm willing to hand it back."

I felt a bit confused. What a sick thing to collect. I knew I had to keep a tough demeanor with that guy if I wanted to keep him open. "Yeah, man, that would be perfect."

He nodded and went back behind the counter, disappearing into a room I couldn't even tell was there. The door was covered in posters and shelving to camouflage it from customers. I didn't have to wait long before he emerged with what I assumed was the magnum, wrapped in a cloth.

He set it down on the counter and unwrapped it. I had flashbacks of Keith. Blood. Budd Dwyer. I hated guns, but I knew my options were limited.

"There she be. Just as sexy as you remember her?"

"Sexier."

"You think that's sexy, check this out." He picked up a small flap of paper that was wrapped with the gun. He opened it up and pinched something between his thumb and index finger. "Know what this is?"

I squinted. It was a slug that had been fired. "Is that... the same bullet?"

He smiled. "Pretty sweet, eh? I don't always get the chance to keep these things, but this one went right through and I found it on the floor. Great collector's item, especially with the gun." He leaned in closer to me, as though he had a secret. He spoke in a soft voice. "Especially when they gone through a nigger."

I wasn't surprised by his racism. I looked closer at the slug, and there it was. It was the image from the Rorschach. I didn't have time to think, and I acted completely on impulse. "Hey, since you're being so nice to me, I'd like to return the favor."

He cocked his head slightly. "Whatchu got that I want?"

"I have a number. You call this number, and I promise you that you'll find yourself in a situation where you can make a clean, legal kill."

"Bullshit."

I wasn't entirely sure how this guy would fair with the test, but if it ended up killing him, I didn't see that as a bad thing. He was a piece of shit in my view. "How do you think I ended up here on the day I did? This lady shows you some images. When you follow them, you end up right where you're supposed to be to make a kill."

"That sounds like some hippie bullshit to me. That, my friend, is what normal people call coincidence."

"I thought so at first, too, but the guys I killed here weren't my first. They weren't my last, either."

I could tell he didn't believe me. "I suppose you can prove that?"

"What if I can?"

"If you got some way to prove to me that you've killed someone since that bullet got lodged in my floor, I'll give you the gun back for nothin'."

I felt that force consuming me, that strange, powerful, compelling force I knew was linked to the ink. It felt like I was watching my own life through someone else's eyes. "Follow me."

We walked together out the front door and down the sidewalk, toward my car. I could tell he was more than a little skeptical. "I don't know what you could possibly have, but if you're up to something, I assume you know I'm packin'."

We stopped at my car and I opened the back door. "Louie, I have a feeling you don't go anywhere without a gun." I pointed inside at the garbage bag. "Take a look in there."

As I watched him open the bag and then look inside the pillow case, I expected a reaction. I expected some swearing or a look of fear. He just nodded and stared, unblinking. "Tell ya what, you let me keep this, and I'll give you the magnum and three boxes of shells."

I hadn't really thought about what I was going to do with the head. I could have asked a million questions. Why did he want it? Did he not care who it belonged to? Didn't he want to hear the story? I decided all of that was irrelevant. I didn't really understand why I kept it in the first place, and having it in my car wasn't the smartest of decisions anyway. "Deal."

I followed him back inside. He carried the garbage bag. I did my best to act natural. He handed me the gun and placed three boxes of ammunition on the counter. I picked them up and turned to leave.

"Hold on, man."

I looked back. I would be lying if I said I wasn't nervous.

"You got that number?"

A sense of relief came over me. I wasn't sure why, but the ink wanted Louie. I wrote Judith's number down on a slip of paper and handed it to him. "You won't be disappointed."

He looked at the garbage bag. "Already not. I'll probably call this broad today. Thanks for coming in."

I nodded. "See you around man, take it easy."

The bell rang as I left. I wasn't sure how to feel about the whole thing, but I knew I got rid of some pretty damning evidence, got a gun, and made a referral. I felt like I accomplished what I set out to do, even if I didn't understand it all. I climbed back in my car. It was starting to get late in the day, so I figured I would head over to Claire's storefront. I wanted Judith, and maybe I would get lucky and catch her leaving.

I had no issues finding the Psych Ink building and parked my car in the least conspicuous spot I could find. I held the gun in my hands and waited. I wasn't sure exactly what I was going to do or who I was waiting for. I wanted to start with Judith, but the sight of Claire would have likely evoked a lot of emotion. Anger clouds the mind, and that awareness made me concerned about making an impulsive decision if the opportunity presented itself.

I scanned the parking lot and saw Judith's car. I decided I would wait for her to come out and then follow her. I glanced at the gun in my hands. So many "what ifs." What if I had never attended that press conference? What if Budd Dwyer had never killed himself on television? What if I kept with journalism? The reality was questions like that didn't matter. Life was what it was, and all I could do was the best I could with what I had.

I placed the gun beside me on the passenger seat and waited. Dusk was creeping in and I was getting tired. I waited another hour before something finally happened. Mind you, not what I expected to happen. A beat-up pickup truck pulled in and parked near the establishment. Without even seeing the driver, I knew it was Louie.

Sure enough, he emerged from the truck. He spat on the ground and went in the front door. I had no idea what hours Claire kept, but I found it a bit surprising she would be seeing clients so late in the evening, since she seemed to care about keeping a professional facade. I waited for another hour, figuring once Louie was done, Judith and Claire would go home for the night.

It turned out I was right, or at least partially right. Judith and Louie emerged at the same time. They spoke a bit in the parking lot before going their separate ways. With both of them leaving at the same time, I knew my odds of being spotted were a lot higher. Luckily for me, Louie left first. Once Judith drove away,I started my car and left a short time later.

I stayed a few cars behind her and felt like I hadn't been spotted. After about twenty minutes, I grew concerned. We seemed to be driving aimlessly around the city. I had my mind made up, though—I was going to deal with her. Even if she knew I was following her, I figured she would have to face me sooner or later.

Another twenty minutes went by and Judith didn't seem to have any real direction. I wasn't sure what her game plan was but I felt like she was trying to waste time. I was feeling more awake, but I knew the events of the day were wearing on me. We drove another fifteen minutes with no apparent destination.

When she finally stopped, I knew she had been on to me. She pulled into a seedy motel not far from the abandoned brick building that started it all. I drove past the parking lot and circled the block. I was hoping she would think I gave up my pursuit and let her guard down. By the time I made it back, her car was parked but she wasn't inside.

I debated going in to find out what room she had rented, but I knew places like that weren't very open with customer information. I decided instead to park in the back of the lot and keep an eye on her car. I didn't really think she would actually sleep there for the night. I didn't know her that well, but she didn't strike me as the bed-bug type.

I turned my car off and watched her black sedan. It was dark out by then, and my adrenaline started wearing off. I told myself I would wait another fifteen minutes and then head back to my apartment for the night. Somewhere in those fifteen minutes, I fell asleep in my car.

CHAPTER TWENTY-FOUR

I HAD BEEN WOKEN up in some strange ways before, but never like I was on that day. In a split second, there was a loud noise and extreme pain on the side of my face and head. It took me a second to even realize where I was.

"You like to stalk women, do ya?"

I put my hand against my face; it was warm. I glanced at my hand and saw it was covered in blood. The driver's side window was shattered. The man that was approaching me looked like he did a lot of drugs and hadn't slept in a week.

"You think you can come here and stalk my customers? Fucking rapist motherfucker!" He clearly wasn't looking for a conversation.

He pulled a small pistol from his waistband and raised it toward me. He pulled the trigger once. The bullet hit the door but didn't go through. I still had the magnum in my lap, and without much thought, I lifted it and squeezed the trigger twice. He grabbed his stomach and fell to the ground.

As I peered out the window, I saw a brick laying on the ground. It was the brick from the ink. The man was moaning in pain. "You shot me in the dick!"

I got out of the car and kicked the brick toward my assailant. "Where is she?"

"Fuck you, call an ambulance. You shot me!"

I looked up to see Judith's black sedan speeding toward the exit of the parking lot. I lifted my gun and fired three shots. One hit the back left tire, and I was pretty sure another struck her somewhere on her body as she seemed to lose control of the car for a moment.

I looked down at the man who fired at me. I raised my gun, knowing it only had one shot left. I fired it through his head and painted the parking lot with his brains. My driver's door was still open, so I tossed the gun onto the passenger seat and climbed in. There was broken glass all over my seat, and my face was bleeding significantly, but I only had one thing on my mind. Follow that black sedan.

I started my car and pressed on the gas so hard my tires squealed. I didn't have time to deal with the police, but I figured that they took their time in that area, if they even got a call at all. Nothing seemed to really matter at that moment except getting Judith.

It was apparent pretty quickly she wouldn't be able to drive very long. The tire I shot was on the rim, and sparks were already flying onto the asphalt behind her. By the way the car was swerving, I was fairly certain the second bullet had hit her. I finally felt like I had the upper hand.

She drove four more blocks before pulling into a parking lot. I followed her in and drove right up on her bumper. Her vehicle came to a rest, but it was still running. I grabbed the gun and jumped out, expecting her to take off as soon as I was out of my car. When she didn't, I knew she must have been seriously injured.

I walked up to the driver's seat with a bit of caution but also some nonchalance. I had the gun in my hand and a smile on my face. I looked inside, and it was clear she had been shot in the neck. The driver's seat had some stuffing coming out of it, right under the headrest and she had lost a lot of blood. I pressed the gun against her forehead and she closed her eyes. Tears streamed down her cheeks.

"Why are you doing this?"

When she didn't answer, I squeezed the trigger. She jumped when the hammer struck the empty chamber. She opened her eyes, probably wondering what Hell looked like. It was interesting to see someone realize they were still alive.

"We can do this the easy way or the hard way. Talk to me."

She smiled,her white teeth covered in blood. "I'm going to die either way. Mind you, I'm not the only one."

I could tell she was trying to get under my skin.I didn't want to take the bait, but curiosity got the better of me. "Me? Are you going to kill me, Judith? Who the fuck are you?"

She leaned her head back against the seat and closed her eyes. She took her hand away from her wound, and the blood poured out in a steady flow. "You? Soon enough. Who else took the test?"

Her question caught me off guard. "Louie?"

She started breathing heavier, and I could tell she didn't have long before she passed out. She smiled. I smashed the butt of the gun into her temple, and she slumped over toward the passenger seat. I saw her purse sitting next to her and reached in and grabbed it.

I looked around to see if I had attracted any attention. The parking lot we ended up in seemed vacant. That part of town didn't have a long shelf life for legitimate business owners. I peered into her purse and rooted around a bit. I found a nail file. It would have to do. She may have looked dead, but I didn't even trust her with that. I slammed the file into the side of her neck that didn't have the bullet wound. Blood poured out as soon as I pulled it out, and she didn't move. She was dead.

For good measure, I stabbed it into her chest a few times and left it protruding about two inches. I figured the scene was obviously a homicide, anyway, and I may as well add some confusion to potentially buy some extra time. If the cops were even called, that was. With a mixture of pride and confusion, I headed back to my car with Judith's purse in hand. I wanted to see if she had any identification in her purse that may give me an address, but I knew I needed to get out of the area.

I tried to follow the speed limits and plan my next move. I was stuck on what Judith said before she died. Who else took the test that I would care about? I decided to go to my office and check in. I didn't mean to fall asleep in a motel parking lot, and Soph was probably worried about me.

Soph. Fuck, she didn't take the test, did she? I knew I had specifically told her not to, but I didn't give her much of an explanation as to why. I found myself driving faster as I thought about the grim possibilities. I wouldn't be able to live with myself if something happened to her.

It took me a few minutes to get to the office. I parked and took a minute to reload the gun. I slid Judith's purse under my arm and put my coat on to conceal the blood on my shirt. I walked with purpose into the building. The closer I got, the more my stomach went into knots. I had too much time to think on the drive over, and too many pieces fell into place that pointed at Sophia. The alternative was Judith was full of shit, but I would never get that admission from her personally.

I turned the handle and hoped I would find it locked. It wasn't. I took a deep breath. If nothing had happened, I didn't need to barge in looking frantic and put my assistant in a panic. I opened it and stepped inside. Sophia was sitting at the administration desk, facing the window. Her dark hair draped over the back of the chair.

"Hey, Soph."

She didn't answer.

"You still upset with me?"

Still no response.

"Soph?" I noticed a foul smell.

The feeling returned to my stomach. I approached her slowly, calling her name. I reached over and grabbed her shoulder, spinning the chair. My eyes widened when I saw what was really there. It was Curtis's face. No, it was his entire head. Sophia had been decapitated and scalped. Curtis's head was haphazardly sewn to her neck, and her hair was stapled to the top of the rotting cranium.

I felt myself go numb. Why her? Why did she have to call Judith? There was no doubt in my mind who was responsible; not many people had been in possession of Curtis's severed head. The anger took over and I kicked in the door to my office with the gun drawn. No sign of Louie.

I checked all the closets and under the desk. I was alone. I went back to the waiting room and locked the front door. Looking over at what was left of my friend, I felt nauseous. It was my fault. On every level, I was to blame. Sophia got involved through Melody, and I personally gave Louie the number.

My trust in fate was gone. My trust in the Rorschach was gone. It was never supposed to get to that point. I had a hard time wrapping my head around how quickly my life became unraveled as soon as Claire was back in it. Claire. She had to die. She could take those fucking tests with her to the grave, and they could predict the Devil's future together in Hell.

I put my hands on the desk and draped my head down. I noticed a slip of paper that had writing that wasn't Sophia's. It was an address. My rollercoaster of emotions came to a screeching halt as I stared at the specific mix of numbers and letters. 314 Elgin St. I wasn't familiar with the area.

I took Judith's purse, which I had nearly forgotten I still had clutched under my arm. I poured the contents onto the desk and saw a wallet. The address was the same. Why would Louie leave me Judith's address? My initial instinct was it was a trap, but with the images in the ink it was never that straightforward.

I tried to compose myself and come up with a plan. I had a long enough trail of bodies behind me I knew my time would be limited. I needed to get Claire, but I couldn't let Louie get away with what he did to Sophia. I looked down at her and tears formed in my eyes. I knew I didn't have time for weakness or mourning. I would have enough time for that in jail or wherever I ended up when the dust settled.

I left the note and packed up Judith's purse. I kept her ID handy so I wouldn't forget the address. I figured if Louie came back for any reason to see if I had discovered the scene, he would think I hadn't when he saw things were still where he left them. I took a deep breath and tried to act normal before heading back to my car.

The first thing I noticed was the smashed out driver's side window. Another reminder of the fact the clock was ticking. Part of me felt like going to Judith's place was a stupid move. Louie didn't strike me as the most intelligent, but I had no idea what he was capable of when it came to planning a murder. He seemed to have some pretty vast knowledge on the subject.

Despite my disdain for the Rorschach, I decided to just start driving and see where I ended up. Whatever forces that were at work were hard to deny, and despite my frustrations and skepticism, I needed some guidance. I had nowhere else to turn. I drove for a few minutes and made a couple turns. I didn't really know where I was going, but before I knew it, I was on Elgin Street.

A couple more blocks and I was sitting out front of the address. I could tell from the road that the front door had been kicked in. Whatever I was walking into, it was apparently the action I was supposed to take. I couldn't understand my devotion after my entire life had been ruined. Maybe it wasn't devotion; maybe it was slavery. Either way, I prepared myself to enter the house.

CHAPTER
TWENTY-FIVE

I APPROACHED WITH CAUTION, my gun loaded and at the ready. I wasn't sure what I was walking into, so I tried not to touch anything. I pushed the barrel of the gun against the door. It was already mostly open, but I wanted to get the best view possible of what was going on inside.

I crossed the threshold slowly and looked around. Everything appeared to be in order. I took another two steps inside, doing my best to move in silence. My heart felt like it stopped when the door frame exploded right above my head. The sound was deafening, and there was no doubt it was a gunshot. I looked to see Louie emerging from the kitchen.

"You know me, boy. I don't miss unless it's on purpose."

As soon as I laid eyes on him, my blood started to boil. "What the fuck did you do to Sophia?"

He curled his upper lip. "That pretty little assistant of yours? Is that a trick question?" He raised his gun at eye level. "Put that gun on the floor."

I felt like I was at an obvious loss. The last thing I wanted to do was give up my only source of protection. "Why? So you can shoot me?"

"If I was gonna shoot you, boy, you'd be dead already. I know you hatin' right now, and I've had a lot of time to think. We goin' old school. Bare hands, no guns."

"Why did you kill Sophia?"

He laughed and snorted. "You was right, boy. Take those tests and you get to kill people. Take this instance right here. You broke into Judith's apartment. She'll be home in a while to discover the scene. She'll call the cops and pretend she don't know nothin'."

"I wouldn't count on that."

"Why? Where's Judith?"

"Is that a trick question?" I smiled to get as deep under his skin as I could. It was working, but I wasn't sure if that was a good thing or not.

"You got two seconds to drop that piece before I shoot it out of your hand."

"What are you getting out of this? Did Claire manipulate you too? She does it with ease, especially with people who... lack intelligence."

He fired another shot, and I could feel it fly past my ear. "Claire's my girlfriend. That was your last warning shot. Next one'll kill you."

I dropped my gun. "Claire is a whore. She's using you."

His response was loud but involved no spoken words. He tossed his gun onto the couch and charged at me with the appearance of a vengeful gorilla. I didn't have much time to react before he pushed me to the ground and started beating on me. His blows came quickly and had quite the force behind them.

"You never say that about Claire." He continued to strike me as he spoke. Little bits of spittle flew from his mouth, and his crooked yellow teeth showed. His breath was almost as unbearable as the pain.

He began to let up, and I found myself staring at the ceiling. I knew I was bleeding and my face was starting to swell. He perched himself on my chest and spit on me. "Well, boy, you ready to die?"

I had a moment of clarity. I hadn't changed my clothes since Melody's apartment. I slid my hand into my pants pocket. I could feel the syringe still waiting there. I pulled it out slowly as I tried to keep him distracted. "What did she promise you?"

"A life. She has power, you know that."

I slid the orange cap off with my thumb, and in a swift motion, I plunged the needle into his neck. I depressed the plunger before he could react, and his eyes rolled back in his head. I had never seen anyone overdose before, but I knew that syringe had been filled with that exact purpose in mind.

He fell limp, still partially on top of me. I rolled him off and stayed on the floor for a few minutes to catch my breath. I sat up and ran my hand over my face. I was bleeding from somewhere. I glanced over at Louie; he was turning a blue-purple color. It looked like he was still breathing, his chest was moving. Shallow breaths.

I got to my feet and looked around for something to wipe the blood off my face. I didn't want to leave any evidence, but I figured it would be best not to go out in public looking like a cage fighter. I grabbed a dish towel from the kitchen and pressed it hard against my forehead. I gathered my thoughts and figured out my next move.

I assumed going back to the office or my apartment were both off the table. Surely the police wanted to talk to me about one thing or another. The way I saw it, I only had one more thing to do. I needed to kill Claire. I picked up my gun and headed back to my car. It was time to go to Psych Ink and find out what the future really held.

CHAPTER TWENTY-SIX

As I DROVE, I could feel my hands shaking on the wheel. I wasn't sure how I felt. I was a bit anxious, a bit scared, and maybe even a bit excited. Whatever happened next was going to end my nightmare. At least I hoped it would. The closer I got to Claire's office, the more my stomach twisted. My breathing was getting so heavy I had to try to regulate it.

I pulled into the parking lot and sat there for a minute. I made sure the gun was loaded before sliding it down the front of my pants and getting out of the car. I pushed my shoulders back a bit to try to relax my body, but the tension was still fairly evident. I didn't want to attract any attention, but I knew I looked like I had just been in a fight.

I had never actually been inside Psych Ink before, so I had no idea what to expect. I pulled the gun out as I opened the front door with as much caution as I could manage. I crept inside, but with the daylight hours, there weren't many shadows to conceal myself in. The office was small. There was a desk and a few chairs in the main room. It almost reminded me of my office and made me think about Sophia.

I did my best to creep around with stealth. I didn't see Claire in the main room, so I figured she must have been behind one of the two doors that lined the room. I knew she was there; I could feel her presence. I could smell her aura.

"You really don't need the theatrics, Lucas. I'm right here."

I turned to my left, and there she was. It was a good thing she didn't have any plans to kill me because I completely missed her sitting in the corner.

"Game's over, Claire."

She stood and took a few steps toward me. Her hair looked darker than the last time I had seen her. "The Rorschach says when it's over, Lucas. You know that."

"Fuck that test."

"That has been your problem since day one. You don't have faith. Has the ink not predicted your fate enough times that you've come to believe?"

I pulled the hammer back, pointing the gun at her face. "There is no fate but that which we make for ourselves."

She smiled and took a step closer, the gun nearly caressing her cheek. "Is that so?"

"You think the ink wants you dead?" I locked eyes with her and pressed the barrel into her skin.

Her eyes were vacant. She showed absolutely no fear, even with a magnum pressed to her face. "Maybe."

"And you're okay with that? Are you really willing to die over this like some kind of martyr?"

She took a couple steps back from me. "I'm not *some* kind of martyr, Lucas. I'm the *legitimate* kind of martyr. Ever since I took my first test, I knew that the ink was my future. I knew I would do anything it asked me to do. I didn't want to leave you. I've never wanted to hurt you, but I can't ignore instruction."

I could tell she was trying to play off my sensitivities, but I didn't know how she could still think I had an attachment to her. "You know how many people have told me that Claire is their girlfriend?"

"Politics, Lucas. You think you fell into that category?"

"I know I did."

She stepped closer to me again, staring right through me. "It's been you and me since the beginning. We both felt it, and I know you believe it."

"I know this test fucks with my head. I know you bring chaos into my life. Why have all these innocent people had to die? Babies died, for Christ's sake."

She shrugged as though my words had no impact. "Who knows. Hitler was a baby once. How many people say that if they could travel back in time they would kill baby Hitler? How do you think that would be seen?"

"A baby is innocent, Claire. It hasn't had time to grow up and become a monster."

"If you put your trust in the Rorschach, you would see that it knows exactly what it's doing. You can kill me, Lucas, but it won't stop the ink. It lives forever. It always has, but most people aren't able to see it."

I lowered the gun and turned away from her. I knew I had gone way past the point of no return. I took a few steps toward the front door, giving her the impression I was leaving.

"I love you, Lucas."

Her words bounced around inside of my head like a superball coated in thumb tacks. Somewhere deep inside of me I really wanted to believe her, and I wasn't sure why. The rest of me wanted to kill her. I raised the gun again and pointed it at her. "Fuck the Rorschach. Gangster rap made me do it." I squeezed the trigger.

The bullet hit her right above her left eye, and she got a strange look of tranquility on her face. She dropped to the ground and lay still. I knew she was dead, but I still didn't feel like it was over. I approached her slowly and kneeled down beside her. I rolled her over enough to see her face. A smile was stretched across her lips. No life in her eyes.

I felt a little indifferent. Her corpse looked more content than I had ever seen one look. I wondered if she had known her death was imminent. That's when it hit me I hadn't seen the last sign. I wanted to convince myself that with Claire not holding the strings the puppet was dead, but somehow it didn't feel like it.

One thing I knew for sure was I had to get out of that building. Gunshots weren't exactly discreet. I left as casually as I could and didn't look back. I decided to head out on foot and see where things went. I wandered around for over an hour, searching the streets in a panic at any sound of a siren. I figured I would just keep wandering until I finally got arrested. Maybe I could pretend to be in a fragile mental state and get some lenience. Maybe I was in a fragile mental state.

Almost another hour had passed when the answer jumped right out in front of me. It was a black squirrel. It paused on the sidewalk and almost seemed to try and connect with me. It was the exact little rodent from the ink. It was the last thing I wanted to see, but at the same time, it was exactly what I had been looking for.

It took off down the sidewalk and followed it. It would get ahead of me, then it seemed to stop to let me catch up. I debated putting a bullet in it just to make a statement. If the Rorschach, or the universe, or whatever, was playing games with me, I was right on the edge of flipping the board over and walking away.

I must have followed that squirrel for twenty minutes before I recognized where I was. It was the seedy part of town I had been to on more than one occasion. When the little bastard ran up the downspout of the old red brick building, I shook my head. I should have known things would come full circle.

The small neon light was back on the façade of the building. "Fortunes told." Half of the letters were burned out or flickering, just as I remembered it. I could see the red Christmas lights illuminated from inside. I took a deep breath. I had come too far and had nowhere else to go. The door was slightly ajar, as it had been back in 1987. I pushed on it and went inside.

CHAPTER TWENTY-SEVEN

THE ATMOSPHERE FELT THE same as I remembered it from all those years ago. The red lights cast a strange shadow on the gypsy, who sat in the same chair behind the same table. It was like a terrible, lucid dream. I felt like I was a young journalist again, seeking guidance from the least likely source.

"Hello, Luke. Been a long time. Did you follow the black squirrel?"

"Yes, Alice. I followed the black squirrel. And it's Lucas now."

"My name is not Alice, it is Esmerelda."

I felt a lot of things, but they all boiled down to apathy. I didn't care anymore. What did I have to care about?

"You have come for a reading?"

"I'm not sure why I've come. Maybe to kill you."

She laughed and leaned forward enough that I could see her face. She had a scar just above her left eye. It was a bullet wound. I took a step closer and squinted a bit. The scar was in the same place I shot Claire. The more I saw her features, the more I realized it was Claire I was looking at.

"It's not possible. You're dead. I killed you."

"Luke, it has been many years. I feel you are confused."

"Cut the shit, Claire. How are you here?"

She leaned back in her chair, concealing her face again in the red shadows. "I am much more than any human. Claire is dead, as you mentioned. I am Esmerelda. Surely by now you have realized the power of the ink. Surely it is that same power that has led you here. Surely you don't think that the power can ever be stopped? It continues on beyond any single human existence."

I felt frozen. I tried to wrap my head around her words. "What the hell have you done to my life?"

"I have done nothing. The universe dictates who it will recruit to intervene with the living. It chose you, Luke."

"Fuck that. I'm not a puppet. I lived my own life and I made my own decisions."

"Then why do you blame me? Is it possible that you believe in divine force only when things go awry? When things happen in your favor you take the credit?"

"I blame you for putting that fucking test in my life. I blame you for whatever the hell got into Claire's head." I lifted my gun and fired a shot. It went right through the gypsy.

"You cannot kill me, Luke. You need to decide what it is that you believe. If you think it's all nonsense, then the Rorschach is nothing more than a vial of ink and three scraps of paper. Claire acted on her own free will, and you are a murderer."

I felt like I was trying to answer an impossible riddle. She was right.

"If you think there is validity, then why don't we do what you came here to do."

I wanted to plead ignorance, but the reality was I knew she was right. I was compelled once again by forces I couldn't explain. I knew I needed guidance to finish my journey, no matter where I was going. Without another word, I held out my hand. She took it in hers and we locked eyes.

It was surreal sitting there next to Claire only hours after I shot her in the face, seeing the wound up close, healed as though it was an old battle scar. Her eyes were dark, but hints of hazel still pierced through and I swore I could see remnants of her soul.

She poked my finger with a small blade and kept her focus on me as she dripped it into the small opening of the inkwell. It felt like some kind of statement. She had done it enough times she didn't even have to see what she was doing. I wasn't sure who I was really looking at. I knew it couldn't really be Claire. But if it was someone else, had she used me to get a new vessel?

The room remained silent as she dripped a single spot of ink onto each paper. I kept my eyes on hers for a moment after she was finished.

"You don't want to see?"

I sighed. "I don't know." I glanced down at the first image. I couldn't tell what it was. It looked like a strange shadow looming on a wall.

The second was undeniable; it was a television camera.

The third was a man shooting himself in the head.

It brought me right back to 1987, toBudd Dwyer shooting himself in front of the media. It didn't make sense. In the dark ink, it was impossible to see the face of the man with the gun. I put my hands over my face and closed my eyes tight. I tried to think of what to say, what to ask, or how to establish some sort of clarity.

I sighed loudly, and after about a minute, I moved my hands. Claire was gone, and so was the Rorschach. The red lights cast a shadow on the wall, detailing part of my head. It was the first image.

I felt a sense of anxiety sweep over me. I had so many unanswered questions, and the only person that could satisfy them had just vanished two feet away from me. I stood and looked around the room. It Looked like an abandoned building in a seedy part of town. There was nothing. I could hear sirens in the distance.

I knew the end was near, and I didn't want the Rorschach to get the best of me. It didn't have the power to create my fate. I alone was in control of my destiny. I ran. I ran from the building and toward the bridge, which is right about the same place I am now. Right where we started.

Now that you know a bit about how I got here, maybe it makes a bit more sense. Though I am looking down at the traffic, and I am debating a swan dive, I am not suicidal. I've never believed in suicide, but maybe if I can avoid the last two images I can somehow break the chain. Destroy the ink by ducking my fate.

"Where the fuck is Claire?"

I recognize that voice. I turn to see Louie. As usual, he's pointing a gun at me. "Is that... a trick question?" I smile.

"You son of a bitch. Turn around and face me. Cops are lookin' all over for you, and we got unsettled business."

I pull my legs up over the edge and dangle them over the road. I'm still sitting on the ledge of the overpass, and the sirens are echoing through the air. "I thought you overdosed?"

He fires a shot, and I feel my kneecap explode. I fall off the barrier and onto the street. I can see police cars closing in, sirens blaring. It looks like media trucks speeding to the scene as well. I can't move; the pain in my leg is agonizing.

"Where the fuck is she?"

I pull my gun from my pants and lift it. "She's dead." I squeeze the trigger, and a single round strikes Louie in the chest. He pauses for a moment, and I swear I can see his life force spill from his eyes. He drops to his knees before face planting into the asphalt.

My sudden act of violence causes the police to spring from their cars before they even completely stop moving. I must have ten guns pointed at me.

"Drop it!"

I lift the gun into my line of sight. "Don't, don't, don't, this will hurt someone."

I glance to my left and see the media closing in, cameras already rolling. A specific young journalist catches my attention. Not so much for the way he looks, but for his camera. It's the same one I saw in the ink. Things are becoming as clear as they can. I place the Model 19 .357 Magnum against my head.

"Please, please, please leave if this will... if this will affect you."

Fucking Budd Dwyer. I squeeze the trigger.

About The Author

Aaron Lebold is an author of psychological horror, sometimes dabbling in extreme elements. His love of the genre began at an early age with all the best slasher films. Writing has always been something of interest but he didn't make any serious attempts at it until 2017. Since that time he has completed several novels and novellas. His short stories can be found in various anthologies by various publishers. Some of his short stories have been narrated for the Cryo-Pod Podcast. His novel "Born Sick" took second place at the Godless 666 awards for best novel of 2022.

Publisher's Note

Thank you for reading Rorschach by Aaron Lebold. We appreciate your support.

If you enjoyed this book, please consider leaving a review on Amazon, GoodReads, or your favorite social media platform.

Broken Brain Books is an indie publisher dedicated to helping authors share their stories with readers around the world. Please visit our website for more information about our releases and signed copies of our books. www.brokenbrainbooks.com

Also Available by Broken Brain Books
Mine by LM Kaplin
Fang Fiction by LM Kaplin
Ruby's Cube by Lyla Diamond

Anthologies by Broken Brain Books
Screams From The Ocean Floor
Screams From Beyond The Veil
Books of Horror Indie Brawl Anthology